ALSO BY SAM PINK

Rontel
Person
The No Hellos Diet
Hurt Others
The Collected Suicide Notes of Sam Pink
Frowns Need Friends Too
I Am Going to Clone Myself Then Kill the Clone and Eat It
No One Can Do Anything Worse to You Than You Can
The Self-Esteem Holocaust Comes Home

Lazy Fascist Press
an imprint of Eraserhead Press
205 NE Bryant Street
Portland, Oregon 97211

www.lazyfascistpress.com

ISBN: 978-1-62105-134-3

Copyright © 2014 by Sam Pink

Cover Art Copyright © 2014 by Sam Pink

Cover Design by Matthew Revert
www.matthewrevert.com

Edited by Cameron Pierce

All rights reserved. No part of this book may be reproduced or transmitted in any form or by any means, electronic or mechanical, including photocopying, recording, or by any information storage and retrieval system, without the written consent of the publisher, except where permitted by law.

All persons in this book are fictitious, and any resemblance that may seem to exist to actual persons living or dead is purely coincidental. This is a work of fiction.

Printed in the USA.

Witch Piss

A novel by Sam Pink

Lazy Fascist Press
Portland, Oregon

IN THE DOORWAY OF AN ABANDONED BUILDING

There was this guy who lived in the doorway of an abandoned building near me.

And we'd become friends.

I saw him whenever I was out walking around trying to avoid my room or find a job.

Every time I walked by, he'd smile and wave and say, "Oh hey"—always in a good mood and willing to talk.

He had a couple blankets and a backpack and some cups.

I don't know, I guess I liked him because he was like, "I live in a doorway but I'm still in a good mood, hey." (He never actually said that, I just thought he might.)

Plus I had no friends.

One night when I passed by the doorway, he sat wrapped up in his blanket, arguing with someone on the sidewalk.

"I'll get money from someone, watch," said the guy in the

doorway. "Someone will give me a dollar. Screw off, man." When he saw me, he held out his hand. "Hey man, c'I please get a dollar?"

"Yeah," I said. "I was just going to say, you want some food? Some beers?"

"Yeah man, please. Would you?"

The person he'd been arguing with stared at me.

"Alright, be right back," I said. "What do you want?"

The guy in the doorway laughed. "What's the limit?"

"Whatever you want. Have some beers with me, man."

"No beer," he said. "Seagram's."

He said it like "Theegram's"—tongue through his missing front teeth.

"Gin or whiskey?" I said.

But he'd started arguing with the other person again. "Screw off man," he said, making a 'shoo/get out of here' motion with his hands.

"Be right back," I said.

The guy in the doorway said, "Hey man, thanks," and held out his fist.

I hit my fist against his fist.

The person he'd been arguing with followed me when I left.

It made my neck itch and I felt pissed.

Inside the 7/11, I watched through the window as he gave me one last look above the ads, continuing down the sidewalk.

Fuck you.

I grabbed a King Cobra 40oz. and asked the cashier to get me a plastic pint of "Dmitry" gin from behind the counter.

Couldn't remember if the guy said gin or whiskey.

Felt like gin was wrong.

Wrong wrong wrong.

Everything wrong!

Back outside, the homeless guy was crossing the street, coming towards me with his blanket wrapped around him.

Cars sped around him, honking.

"Motherfuck!" he said, dodging the last car and hopping onto the sidewalk.

"Boom," I said, handing him the pint. "Sorry, I forgot, did you say gin or what?"

"Nah, not gin," he said, then smiled and waved his hand. "But anything's fine, man. Thanks. I'm just glad that fucker's gone, haha. Fuckin asshole son of a bitch. Hate that guy."

"I thought he was your friend when I came up. I didn't know."

"Nah, I asked him for money and he said yeah at first but then started giving me shit about how I should have a job, and how I'm physically fine, and this that and the other bullshit. I'm like, 'Let's see you spend five years in my shoes, bud. Try it.'"

"Yeah, fuck him," I said, smiling. "Hate that guy."

I decided then to only ever encourage people, no matter what they wanted to do.

To get through life by saying yes to everything, so no one could say I didn't get what I wanted, and also so nobody would dislike me.

The homeless guy opened the door of the 7/11. "Let me get some soda from the place here. They give me free soda."

Thoda.

Free thoda.

He was holding the door for me.

"No," I said. "I was just in there."

So I waited outside.

Thoda.

Thoda thoda thoda.

Smelled like it was going to rain.

Rain down your worst rain, you bastard-ass motherfuckers, I thought, squinting at a vague area across the street.

Yeah.

Yeah, drown me.

Kill me, come on.

The homeless guy came back out and poured the gin into the plastic cup.

We started to cross the street with the stoplight still yellow, but I stopped halfway for a car approaching.

Homeless guy said, "Don't worry"—pulling on the shoulder part of my shirt.

But I stayed back and so did he, and the car sped through the light.

The force pushed my clothing against me.

"Fucker blew right through that shit, see that?" he said, watching the car. "Holy fuck, haha."

"Yeah, shit," I said, smiling.

I imagined how my body would've reacted to the collision.

Maybe like, shot backwards into the air where my spine breaks at the waist and my heels kick my own head and then I open back up until my toes kick my face and it repeats until I'm gone up into the sky.

A perfect departing.

A goodbye kiss like I mean it!

"Yeah, so that guy was saying how no one would help me, and this that and the other fuckin shit. I mean, I'm not going to work some bullshit job for three dollars an hour like a fuckin immigrant. I'm a citizen. Fuck that. I'm American."

"Yeah man," I said, undoing the cap on my 40. "Fuck him." I took a pull, put my bottom lip over my moustache area and sucked foam out of the hair. "Let's go find him and kill him."

The guy laughed and got back into his doorway.

I stood on the sidewalk and talked to him as he sat there staring out at the street, hood over his head, blanket wrapped around him like a tepee.

He talked about the various Chicago neighborhoods he'd lived in.

"Yeah, Little Village is real nice," he said. "Humboldt Park too. Oh yeah, but I'd a problem with a group of people around here, though. They're called cops."

He said "cops" like "copth."

"Fucking pigs," he yelled out into the street, retching at the end of the yell.

I laughed, took a pull off my 40.

Just wanted to drink until I was brave enough to get into a dumpster and hide beneath some bags.

To be collected and crushed with all the other garbage.

All the same.

Take me with, I thought.

I looked across the street and saw some paper blowing around the gutter.

Take me with.

It was the part of summer when temperatures drop at night and it gets kind of cold.

And you can think things and not admit them to anyone else, and that's what makes those things so good.

Like what if there is an exact amount of this very 40 that I could drink—and not exceed—to make me soundlessly and painlessly disappear.

Things like that.

Things that seem sometimes possible but only at certain times, and only if you didn't tell anyone.

Because your thoughts are all you have.

I don't know, fuck it.

The guy in the doorway adjusted his blanket tepee. "Man," he said, laughing. "Those fucking cops, they push me around, fuckin punch and kick me n'shit. Hate those fuckers."

Fuckerth.

"Motherfuckers," I said, grinding my teeth.

And I meant it.

Imagining myself enlarged, inhaling the smoke off a burning cop as he screamed "no no no"—unable to even touch his agonizing face because his skin's so blistered.

Chicago Police.

Murderers, torturers, gangbangers.

Die and go to hell, you motherfuckerth.

Just kidding/everyone makes mistakes!

Thoda thoda thoda.

"Yeah but, I can live here no problem," he said, "I know the guy who owns the building. I thweep the block for him every couple days. Private property, motherfucker"—waving at some imaginary person. "Thee ya."

"Fuck yeah," I said, looking at the doorway. "This is really nice."

I squatted and took a pull off my 40.

People passed on the sidewalk.

He asked them for money.

"Hey sweetheart," he said, to a girl with a big ass.

She said hi, smiled at us as she passed.

I took a pull off my 40, waving to her.

And we were there for each other.

For however many seconds, we completely justified each other.

"It's nice out," I said.

The guy in the doorway said, "Hey, yeah, that's ok buddy, because I gotta hit the bed anyway."

He held out his hand through an open flap in the tepee.

I looked at him for a second.

"Oh, ok," I said. "Night, man."

We shook hands and locked thumbs.

He lay down, curling up under his blanket.

I walked off, drinking the rest of my 40.

Imagining myself in the homes I passed.

Using the furniture.

Walking from one room to the next.

Smelling the kitchen.

Sleeping in the bedrooms.

Hearing the sounds.

Touching the walls.

Why not.

My 40 was down to the bottom eighth.

Mostly backwash.

Witch piss.

I threw it into a dumpster behind a gas station and walked

the rest of the way with my hands in my pockets and my head down.

A nice method.

Ah yes, very very nice.

By my apartment this rat came out from beneath a car and ran down the alley.

Gone.

Take me with.

Things like that.

Things that seemed possible but only if you were desperate enough.

DANNY, DUKE, SPIDER-MAN, AND EVERYONE ELSE AT THE WIG PARTY

Next time I walked by the doorway there were a bunch of guys there, and also a dog lying on the sidewalk.

Everyone except the dog was wearing a wig.

They all introduced themselves, starting with the guy who lived in the doorway, who said, "Eyyyy, you remember me, right? I'm Danny."

But he'd never told me his name.

So it was Danny, Troy, who just stood up and walked away drunk, Spider-Man, Too Tall, and another guy sitting in the doorway holding a leash on Duke (the dog).

Danny's friends.

Listening to the radio and wearing wigs.

"What's good, man?" I said, slapping hands with Danny.

He had a blanket over his legs, drinking fruit-flavored malt liquor.

"Shit, just drinking," he said. "Lissnina Sox game."

Thox.

The Thox game.

Said they'd been celebrating earlier for some other guy's birthday.

Which meant he had more friends than me.

And a better social life.

And more wigs.

This one guy—Spider-Man—he tapped my arm and touched his blue-tinsel wig.

He laughed, raspy.

"Ey, aren't ch'gon ask about my beautiful hair?" he said. Then, a little quietly, he said, "Y'gotta be kiddin me"—giving me a look that meant "Y'gotta be kiddin me."

"Yeah, what is this shit?" I said, touching his wig.

Danny laughed, ashing his crooked handrolled cigarette.

He was wearing a black-haired wig sideways, bangs on one side and long curls on the other—his toothless smile and gray-stubbled cheeks laughing beneath.

He said, "Somebody left me a bag with some sweaters and some wigs in it this morning."

"Somebody left you wigs?" I said.

"Yeah, thith morning," he said.

He laughed, tongue through his missing front teeth.

Everyone else laughed.

Spider-Man yelled, "Wig time! Wha's really goin on? Woo!"

Duke stretched his legs out on the sidewalk and licked his lips.

I wanted to grab Duke by the cheeks and kiss the top of his head, holding my lips against his head for a little while, going, 'mmmm' then 'whaa!' when I finally released the kiss.

Duke, who loves ya!!!

"What do you guys want from the store?" I said. "I'm going."

Everyone said yeah, and get this, get that.

"I'm just getting a case of beer," I said. "What about Duke.

Does he need anything?"

Spider-Man yelled, "DUUUUUKE!"

Duke lifted his head off the sidewalk, licking his lips.

The owner barely had his eyes open, rubbing his face.

He took off his wig and set it on Duke's head, but it slid off immediately.

"Nah, Duke's good," he said. "He just sleepy from walking around all day."

"No, I'll get him something," I said. "What does he need?"

"Ok. Some treats, I guess."

"Yeah," I said, nodding.

Yeah, fuck yeah.

Everybody needs treats.

I went to the 7/11 and got a 30-pack of beer and some dog treats.

The dog treats were designed to look and taste like bacon.

The package had a crazy-looking cartoon dog on the front, its tongue hanging out the side of its mouth, eyes sticking out.

Fuck yeah.

Duke, are you even ready for this shit?

Back at Danny's, I gave everyone a beer—except Danny, who wouldn't drink anything except his watermelon-flavored malt liquor.

I gave Spider-Man a beer.

"Hayo yeah," he said. "Thanks, du." He opened the beer and took a pull. "Mmm! Spicy! Ey so I went and saw [recently released comic book superhero movie] again. Maaaaaan, gah be kiddin me, woo! Fuckin amazing. Fuckin bananas."

He talked about the movie, which everyone but me had seen.

Most of them had seen newly-released movies at least once.

They celebrated birthdays, had get-togethers, saw movies, owned pets/wigs.

Jealousy.

The burning jealousy.

"Luh that movie," said the guy standing next to me.

Too Tall.

Too Tall was wearing a wig of like, silver/old-lady hair.

He had on a huge T-shirt and corduroy pants and Velcro shoes.

He was only a little taller than me and everyone else there, with a big stomach.

He'd just been standing with his hands and back against the building, humming to himself.

I handed him a beer.

"Man, shoot," he said, smiling. "Thanks enough, jo."

He opened the beer and finished it in two pulls.

Spider-Man did little dances for people who passed by on the sidewalk, letting his long tinsel wig flip around in front of his face and mumbling, "Y'gah be kiddin me."

Too Tall gestured at Spider-Man with his can and said, "Ey, that man, shoot, he a great artist. F'I had some money, I mean, when I get my break, I'ma support him. Because what he do, he great."

Too Tall put his can on the ground and stomped it, catching the gray wig before it fell off his head.

I put the crushed can into a plastic bag with a few others.

Too Tall said, "Yeah, man. Shoot. He get hisself some paper, he draw anyone that passes. Tell you."

"Gah be kiddin me," said Spider-Man, stopping his dance.

He raised his eyebrows up and down, smiling.

He mimed shooting a basketball, jumping backwards, wig waving.

His clothes—if washed—were nicer than mine.

Plus he had a good attitude and his jumpshot looked better.

Overall, I liked him more than me.

Too Tall said, "He see yo face one time"—splayed his hand over his own face—"an he draw you exactly perfect." Shrugging. "He do."

Spider-Man lit a handrolled cigarette and told me about some comic book characters he'd created.

"Oh, I got heroes, gah be kiddin me." He held one wrist

with the other hand and said, "Ice Man." He was staring straight forward dramatically. He pointed his hand forward, still holding it by the wrist. "Shing shing. Gotta be kiddin me. Got ice powers. Shing shing. Boosh."

He did really good sound effects.

Over 75% of what he was saying was just sound effects.

Doing moves on the sidewalk and shooting ice at imaginary enemies, his wig waving.

He held out one hand in front of his face and made a fist then jumped and turned in the air and went, "Shing shing."

"Some people got sport skills, they do hole-in-ones," Too Tall said, as we both watched Spider-Man perform fight maneuvers on the sidewalk. "Some people smart, they do algebra. But this du, he a artist. He amazin. Tellin you. When I get some money."

Spider-Man said, "Dahhhh. Wha's really goin on?"

Then he gave a brief storyline of one of his characters, which he told with a lot of sound effects.

It involved a dead father and something with ice.

There were other storylines too.

Most of them involved a dead father/wife.

Genetic accidents.

Something with ice.

He posed as the characters while narrating.

At one point he got annoyed when he thought people weren't listening.

From the doorway, Danny yelled, "Then just tell the fuckin story then, the quick version. Come on."

Everybody laughed.

Spider-Man continued to talk about the comic book characters he'd created.

He posed as the fighters and did their moves, pausing for people who walked by, bowing to them as they passed.

He jumped back into fighting position and said, "Shing-shing"—shooting some ice at me.

I dodged as best I could, drinking my beer.

Spider-Man moved strands of the sparkling wig away from his face. "Gotta be kiddin me, my beautiful hair. Dahhhhhh."

This guy 'Face' walked up.

Everybody said hi to him.

He was Spider-Man's friend.

He wore a Sox hat to the left a little, braids coming out beneath it.

There was a long scar on his cheek/jaw.

"Whattup, cous," he said, hitting fists with me when I handed him a beer.

More and more people were passing on the sidewalk.

The bars were closing.

Face said he had to go soon to clean up afterhours at a nearby bar called the Two Door.

This professional/jock type guy walked up and started talking to Duke's owner.

They knew each other.

The jock guy handed him his cellphone.

Duke's owner took out his cellphone and held both phones next to each other, transferring a number.

He sat there moving his head back and forth between both phones, dialing with his burnt fingertips.

"Wha'd you want again?" he said, squinting up at the jock guy.

"Some weed, shit, some coke, whatever," he said. "We can all blow a line right here, I don't give a fuck."

He looked at me for a second and then looked back down at the dog-owner guy.

Nothing.

"Nothing," said the dog-owner guy. "Should I try again, er?"

The jock guy grabbed his phone and walked off.

His sandals slapped against the sidewalk.

I ran across the street and pissed in an alley.

When I came back there was an argument between Danny and Spider-Man about who could ask for money where.

Territories.

Rules.

Power.

Friends or no friends.

Danny kept telling Spider-Man to fuck off because he was asking for money by his spot.

Spider-Man kept telling Danny to relax.

An ad on Danny's radio mentioned the Somethingth Anniversary of 9/11.

Everyone talked about how they would have attacked the terrorists if they were on those planes.

Danny said, "Man, fuck it, you know. Wha'd they have? Fuckin box cutters? A fucking box cutter? Helllllllll"—tongue through his missing teeth—"lll no. I mean, yeah, you cut me once, sure. But then I fuckin kill your ass, haha. Fuckin stomp your face in, bitch."

Too Tall took off his wig and rubbed his head. "Mm-hm. Can't stop me with jussa box cutter."

Face put his cigarette in his mouth and held both his fists clenched down at his sides, squinting around the smoke. "Bitch-ass motherfuckers, come on," he said, acting like he wanted to fight Spider-Man.

Spider-Man said, "Gah be kiddin me, come on." He walked over to a parking meter and fought it. "Boosh boosh. Pwah. Shing."

He told a dramatic story about 9/11, how on the plane the passengers downed, this guy called up his wife and said goodbye before helping to attack the terrorists.

Spider-Man kept dramatically reciting one part, posing as the guy and his wife.

"'Baby, baby no, I have to go,' he says to his girl. And his girl, she say, 'Baby please no.' But he says, 'Baby I love you—I have to go.'"

I kept thinking about some of his comic book characters.

Wanted to be able to think of something flawed about their

storyline/superpower, that way I could hurt his feelings.

But I couldn't think of anything.

His characters were too good.

Too damn good!

Spider-Man stopped the 9/11 story, yelling, "Stop, come on, gah be kiddin me," as Danny pretended to shoot ice at him.

"Shing shing *that*, motherfucker," Danny said.

He laughed and grabbed the tallboy can of watermelon-flavored malt liquor near his feet.

"Shing, shing," Face said, shooting ice at Spider-Man.

Everyone was laughing.

Spider-Man walked off, pissed, gone.

"Good," Danny said. "Fuck that whiner."

Everyone else agreed.

And it became clear to me they weren't all friends.

And that nobody was ever friends.

And that yes, fuck that whiner.

We finished up the case of beer.

Duke stretched a little, started to get up.

It took Duke a long time to get up, and when he did, he walked bow-legged and limped.

The owner took him over to a nearby square of dirt where there'd been a tree.

"He got arthritis," said the owner, watching Duke spray dark piss into the dirt and over the sidewalk.

Will the treats help?

Shit, I hope they help.

Yes.

They will.

They will cure him!

They will melt in his mouth and travel down into him, out into his limbs and joints, yelling, "Ey, arthritis, fuckatta here! Told you!"

And Duke will vomit out the defeated arthritis as a green mist, or whatever, and be healthy again.

Healthy and strong Duke.

Large enough to drown Chicago in his dark piss.

Duke, I love you, enjoy the treats, have a nice night.

Mmmm-wha!

I put the plastic bag full of crushed cans into the empty beer case and said bye to everyone and threw the empty beers into a dumpster and went home and slept and I didn't have any dreams.

PIÑA COLADA

The next couple of times I passed by Danny's spot he wasn't there.
Just his plastic cups, his blanket, and some newspaper.
No Danny.
After a couple weeks, the doorway was boarded up.
I didn't find out what happened until I saw Spider-Man one afternoon, singing loudly and crossing the street towards 7/11.
I ran to join him right as the 'Walk' signal turned.
"Ey, you're Danny's friend," I said. "We hung out a while ago. The wig night."
He looked at me for a second then smiled. "Dahhhh, wha's good, man?"
He held out his hand.
We shook, locked thumbs.
"No I mean, wha's *really* good, man?" he said. "Gah be kiddin me, woo!"
"Yeah," I said, smiling. "Nice to see you again."
He had on a Spider-Man baseball hat, tipped back on his head, sweat coming down from his thinning white hair.
T-shirt with a cartoon mouse dressed like Elvis.

Pajama pants with the Bears logo all over them.
Dress shoes.
We stood on the corner out front of the 7/11.
"Where's Danny?" I said. "His place is boarded up."
"You didn't hear, man? Danny got hit by a car, bro. Gah be kiddin me! He got hit by a drunk driver when he's crossing right over there"—pointing at the street that was part of the intersection we'd just crossed. "Motherfucker goes right through the redlight, boosh"—slapping his hands together and sliding them different ways.
"Oh shit."
Spider-Man laughed and said, "Oh shit is right." He backed up a few steps and punched through the air and said, "Fwoosh, ran right into him, man. See that bus stop?" He got really close to me and pointed towards a bus stop a little bit down the block. "He got knocked all the way over to that bus stop. Kiddin me? Shit, thassa a hundred feet bro! Gah be nuts. Fuckin bananas. Bananas *and* nuts, du."
I looked down the block to where Spider-Man was pointing.
Fwooosh.
"Man," I said.
"Yeah, du."
"So where is he? Is he alive?"
"Oh, he with his dad now, up in Arlington Heights. Him and the stepmom. They got money, bro! His dad's uh, um, a retired engineer. Plus, they fuckin suing everybody, man. Gah be nuts. The driver, the police, everybody man."
He backed up, his fists out to his sides as he looked up at the sky, acting out something, grimacing.
"They suing everybody," he yelled, "Naaaaaaaaang!"
I was laughing.
He came closer again and wiped sweat off his forehead. "He got a compressed spine, bro! You kiddin me! Nah, but he's doing ok. His dad don't let him drink now. Locked the motherfuckin booze in the basement with a padlock."

I imagined Danny trying to bite through the padlock for some reason—gnawing on it, then snapping his fingers and saying, "Ah rats."

"Man, lotta accidents happen at this stop right here though," Spider-Man said. "Shit, like, two years ago, I's drinkin a beer over there." He pointed across the street at a bus stop down the block. "Sitting right there, had my beer, ok. Then, fuckin boooosh, fuckin four cars smash into each other, right there man, at the intersection. Gah be nuts. I'm drinkin a beer, and motherfuckers"—he hit his fists together and said, "Cooooooooorrrsh." He backed up, spreading his arms out like he was exploding out of something in slow-motion. "Fuckin bananas. One car goes fuckin airborne, du!" He pointed at the stoplight. "See that bitch right there? It was *that* high, bro. Shit spun over upside down and the other cars smashed into buildings, people thrown out all over. Fucking blood, guts. I got up from the bench, I's like, naaang. This one bitch, she layin there"—pointed to the street—"layin in the gutter, like"—he straightened up with his hands tightly at his sides and his eyes closed then shook his head side to side while vibrating his lips, making an engine/speedboat sound.

"Oh shit," I said.

"Ok?" he said, laughing. He slapped one hand into the other, raised his eyebrows. "Bro, then I found a arm in the street! What!? This one du lossa arm! Gah be nuts! Bananas. Fuckin walnuts, man. Kiddin me?"

He closed his eyes and shook his head.

He folded one arm beneath the other, rubbing his chin with the other hand, still shaking his head side to side like, *Here we go again!*

"And I's just out by the bus stop, drinking my beer," he said, shrugging. "Shit, I'm always first on the scene." He came up to me and showed me a Spider-Man ring on his left ring finger then pointed at his hat. "Spidey's alllllllllways first on the scene, bro. Man, I thought to myself, 'Why's it always me. *Why.*'"

"It's because you're always hanging out," I said.

"Bro, I ran out into the street, see du's arm, fwoosh, I run to the 7/11, run straight the fuck in, go to the back. See that?" He turned me a little by the shoulders and pointed through the 7/11 windows at the ice coolers. "I grab a motherfuckin bag from there, run out without paying, straight out into the fuckin street. Crack the bag open, pour some out, grab du's arm"—he laughed a little—"grab the fuckin arm and tossed it into the bag, shook that shit up, chirsh chirsh."

I was smiling. "Oh shit, man. I wouldn't have thought of that."

"Dahhhhhhhhhh," he said smiling, raising his eyebrows up and down.

Then he did some kind of strut where he carefully lifted and set his feet while pointing downward.

"Did it save his arm?" I said.

"Nah, I don't know. I never seenem again, gah be kiddin me. Fuckin bananas." He calmed down, blinking a little to clear his watering eyes. "Woo. But yeah."

"What if it saved his arm and he always wonders who did it?"

Spider-Man looked at me for a couple seconds.

Maintaining eye contact, he knelt and covered the lower half of his face with his forearm.

In a weird, extra-gravelly voice, he said, "It is what I must do for my city."

"Hell yeah," I said.

He stared at me over his forearm, breathing heavily like, "Sersh...sersh...sersh."

Then he stood and smiled.

"You should've grabbed chips and candy too when you got the ice," I said.

But he didn't hear me.

He was adjusting the brim of his hat, making a face.

"Shit man, then I's in the middle of the street directing traffic! Fuckin blood and glass all over. Dahhh. Shit. I got du's arm in a bag and I'm directing traffic. You serious?" He came up to me and hit my arm. "When the cops finally got there, the one officer's like, 'Thanks, Spidey.'" He hit me again and started laughing. "Waaaayyyooohhh. Wha's *really* going on?"

We both laughed.

A girl walked up to the corner, waiting for the 'Walk' signal.

She had on headphones.

Spider-Man looked at her from bottom to top—holding his one elbow, scratching his beard a little.

He tapped her arm with the back of his hand.

"And how are you doing today?" he said, in an overly polite tone.

She took off one of her headphones and said, "What?"—her eyebrows raised.

Same tone, he said, "And how are you doing today?"

"Fine."

"How's your day going?"

She went to put her headphone back on but stopped. "Fine."

"Well it's supposed to be perfect."

"What?"

He started to say the same thing but she smiled halfway through, put her headphone back on, and walked across the street.

Spider-Man watched her.

"Nang!" he said. "She got a ass!"

He started doing a weird strut again.

A motorcycle sped down the street.

Spider-Man watched it.

"Wooooo," he said. "Thassa bad-ass bike, bro! See how that shit was chopped-out? Nang."

He told me about a comic book character he liked who had a magical motorcycle.

If you mentioned something comic book related, he'd tell you as much as he knew about that character and also jump into the plot of the movie and start acting it out.

"Shit man," Spider-Man said. "[Character] is a bad motherfucker, gah be kiddin me! Du's skin is made of liquid metal.

LIQUID METAL, BRO! Come on!" He made a motorcycle revving motion with his hand. "Gagga gagga, vooosh. He hop on that bike, shit, his skull burst inna flames, furrshhhh. Fuckin nuts."

"Nah, he's a pussy," I said, for no reason, knowing nothing about the character.

Spider-Man laughed. "Dahhhhh. Liquid metal, bro! The fuck!?"

I said, "So what does that mean. Is it like—"

"Bro, that shit is liquid, metal. Fuck a bullet, fuck a knife. Gah be kidding me. Plus his motorcycle goes 700 miles an hour, du. Seven. Hundred. Fucking. Miles an hour, man. Peel that fucking pavement, man. Leave that shit melted. Bike goes so fast, you go up the side of a building." He pointed down the street to where the Sears Tower was visible. "Go up the fucking Sears Tower, no problem. Jump off the top of that bitch and land in the street, fwoooosh, fucking zoom by, flip over all the cars, smash out all the windows. Ooooooosh."

He mimed being exploded backwards out of something, a pained looked on his face.

Then he made a motion like he was taking out a whip, whipping me with the sound effect 'Tish.'

"Du's got a fucking chain-whip too, man," he said. "Fucking rip your head off, son. Tish."

"Oh fuck no," I said.

"Oh fuck *yeah*, du," he said, turning and whipping something else. "Tish."

"What if my skin is made of liquid metal too?" I said.

"Fuckin nuts, bro," he said, lighting a handrolled cigarette. "Fuckatta here."

He talked about an upcoming movie where multiple superheroes were going to be fighting together.

He listed them, doing a pose for each.

"[Character]," he said, then stood straight up and crossed his arms over his chest and said, "Shing, shing."

Then he said, "[Character]" and flexed in a really dramatic

way and said, "Byahhhhh."

Then he said, "[Character]" and acted like he was holding a powerful orb of energy between his curled hands, and said, "Nyah ha haaaaaa."

I said, "Hell yeah, man. Can't fuck with that"—even though I wasn't sure you couldn't fuck with that.

Somebody could probably fuck with that.

Spider-Man stopped and narrowed his eyes at me and listed all the superheroes again, louder but somehow more calm too.

He didn't think I'd truly understood what grouping those superheroes together meant.

And it bothered him.

"Fuck," I said. Then I did a shrug, making a face I'd never made. "They don't have a weakness."

"No weaknesses," he said, smiling. "Dahhhhhh. Fuckatta here."

He backed up and performed a move.

"Fuck with us," he said. "Try it. Go on."

He did an elaborate jumpkick move, landing by someone trying to get past on the sidewalk.

He bowed—remained bowed—using both arms to usher the person onward.

"So, what are you doing today then?" I said.

He straightened up and wiped his nose with the back of his hand, sniffing. "Uh, nothing man, just went out to get some piña colada to drink with my woman."

He told me they lived a block away, in an alley underneath the Blue Line tracks.

"If I can't get piña colada I'll get margarita, fuck it," he said, looking toward the store. "I better go see what they got though. My girl gonna beat my ass. I been gone so long haha. You know what I'm sayin, naaaaang. When I get back, she'a whoop my ass!" He laughed while making a face that could also be used during a guitar solo. "She'a whoop my ass."

75% of conversations in Chicago seemed to involve a whooped ass.

Or an ass that should've been whooped.

An ass that narrowly avoided its whooping.

An ass that wouldn't escape its whooping.

A theoretical ass whooping.

Facts.

Enactments.

"Alright, later man," I said. "I hope they have piña colada."

I put my hand out.

We shook hands and locked thumbs.

"Later," he said, snapping.

He jogged toward the 7/11 to hold the door for someone.

I walked down Fullerton.

There was an ad on the side of a bus that read, 'Every baby will grow up to be somebody important'—showing a baby dressed as a firefighter, one dressed as a doctor, and one as a hamburger.

Actually no, I couldn't see the third one—think it was a judge maybe.

SPIDER-MAN AND JANET AND HAPPINESS INC.

The next day, I went to the alley beneath the train tracks where Spider-Man lived.

He was standing next to a wheelchair, trying on what looked like an official U.S. Air Force shirt.

"Yo!" he said, straightening the arms out on the shirt and examining the patches. "How you like it?"

"Looks good, man," I said.

"Dahhhhhh. Shit's fuckin badass, du. Somebody dropped it off for me last night."

Against a brick wall behind him there were two green recycling dumpsters with a mattress between them, and a tarp pinned down to each dumpster for cover.

I heard someone moving behind it.

There was a younger overweight guy sitting on an overturned bucket against a train track column, silently drawing.

I asked Spider-Man if he wanted some beers.

"Hayo yeah, man, come on," he said. "Come with me." He

patted the guy drawing. "Be back, man."

The guy didn't react at all.

On the other end of the alley there was a carwash exit, freight door open with foamy water pooling out.

We entered the carwash and walked through the big garage area where employees were hand-drying cars.

Spider-Man led me to a door inside the carwash that was the back entrance to a small liquor store where he worked.

Once a week he swept, vacuumed, and took out boxes for five King Cobra 40ozs. and five handrolled cigarettes.

"Yeah, I come over here," he said, walking me around the 10' x 10' liquor store. "Sweep a little, fiss fiss, then I grab those boxes over there, vacuum the carpets, woosh woosh. Presto magnifico."

I bought a tallboy for myself and a 40 for Spider-Man.

We went back through the carwash.

Spider-Man moved his fist and said, "A-ohhhhhhhhh" to the employees.

No one reacted.

We walked out through the big freight door and crossed the alley.

Spider-Man's woman had taken down the tarp.

She was sitting on the bed, staring up, crosseyed.

She had a baseball hat on backwards, her thick tangled black hair coming out all sides.

She wore a Bulls T-shirt and a diaper made of garbage bags, her legs posed in front of her.

She was eating a rolled-up piece of deli turkey, slices stacked on her unshaven thigh.

"This my girl, Janet," Spider-Man said, smiling and gesturing toward her.

"Hi, nice to meet you," I said.

She said, "Um, nice a meet you too. Hi I'm juh, Janet."

She strained when talking, breathless.

"She my girl," Spider-Man said, opening the 40 and smiling at me.

He took a pull.

I grabbed an empty bucket and flipped it over.

I sat and opened my tallboy.

"Here man," Spider-Man said. He went behind a dumpster and came back with a folding chair. "This shit right here, this shit is pure bamboo. Fuckatta here."

He set up the chair, his open Air Force shirt blowing in the wind.

"Thanks," I said, sitting down. "Oh, shit. Nice."

"Pure, 100 percent bamboo," he said, making an 'ok' sign.

Janet said, "Bum boo," chewing turkey with her mouth open. "Hehe, shit. Dayum. Fock dat."

A train passed over us, going towards the California stop.

It was hot out.

Sweat went down my chest into my bellybutton.

The guy who was drawing, he'd look up every once in a while and whisper something to himself, then go back to drawing.

He had a lisp like someone was pinching his lips open a little.

One time he looked up and said something and we made eye contact and he kept looking at me and eventually I said, "What?"

He leaned forward, handing me his drawings.

It was a stack of 'To:/From:' stickers from the post office.

He'd drawn 'Happiness Incorporated' on one, in bubble letters.

Another one said, 'Peace, Love…Happiness Incorporated' in bubble letters.

I handed the stickers back to him.

Janet said, "Um, beb, can you peez hand me uh, the uh, juice, peez. Shit. Dayum."

Spider-Man grabbed a juicebox off the ground and put the straw to her mouth.

She took a sip. "Thuh, thank you, beb."

Spider-Man set the juicebox in her lap.

On the front it had a picture of a neon strawberry and it read: 'Poppin' Strawberry!'

"Aw shit," I said. "Poppin' Strawberry."

Janet bit into some rolled-up turkey.

She smiled. "Shit hehe. Dayum. Fock dat."

Spider-Man said, "Dahhhhh, shit's poppin!" He cleared his throat. "But nah, that's our favorite one. There's that one, then Rockin' Raspberry, and something else. Right babe?"

Janet didn't say anything, just kept chewing.

Spider-Man said, "See man? She don't listen to me. She hate me."

Janet said, "Hey, wuh, watch it"—pointing a roll of turkey at him, her hand shaking.

Spider-Man laughed. "Oh shit. I better hol up. She'a whoop my ass."

Janet smiled. "Thass, ruh, right. Doe fock with me. Shit. Fock dat. I'm Puerto Rican."

She bit into another folded piece of turkey and chewed, her mouth open.

Spider-Man and I laughed.

"She ain playin, man," he said, leaning back on his milk crate chair, back against a dumpster. "Man, I fucked up one time, she ran my ass over with that wheelchair."

I looked at her wheelchair, parked next to him.

It had a huge battery and controls on the armrest.

Spider-Man said, "That shit's heavy, du! She ran over my foot, right over the bones. Hurt like a motherfucker. Member babe?"

Janet nodded, chewing with her mouth open. "Shit. Fock dat."

"But, ey," he said. "That's my girl. I love her. She my doll. You need me, right babe? I help you. Brush your hair. Clean you. I help you."

"Um, jes," she said. "Thank you, beb. Shit. Hehe."

"Man we been together 15 years," Spider-Man said. He leaned back and took a pull off his 40, maintaining eye contact with me. He raised his eyebrows up and down. "15 years, bro! I love her. She gave me my youngest daughter, Yanita."

"How old is she?" I said.

"She 12, but she'a whoop that *ass*, bro." He laughed. "Wooo.

She mean! She with the grandma now but man, she my heart. I love her."

"I'm Puerto Rican," Janet said, pointing to herself with a roll of turkey. "Shit. Dayum."

"Yeah, Janita whoop that ass, man," Spider-Man said. "She in karate. Plus she Puerto Rican. Plus dude, I'm Black/Irish/American-Indian *and* British." Then in a deep, booming burp, he said, "Nang!"

Everybody laughed, even the Happiness Inc. guy, who looked up and said something I couldn't hear.

I took a pull off my tallboy.

Spider-Man told me about how he used to get government money for taking care of Janet and how he will again once he gets his state ID renewed.

Also, once he got any kind of picture ID, he could sleep over at Janet's assisted living apartment.

Janet had a full apartment—shower and everything—but she slept out here in the alley with him because he couldn't get in without an ID.

"Shit, but ey," he said. "She my baby. She even let me bring other women home sometimes, man." He stood up and started pacing. "Hayo yeah, man. We eat other females alive. Like a porno here. Got one lickin the other's pussy while I do one from behind. Takin pictures on my cellphone and shit, what!?"

Janet finished some turkey and wiped her fingers off on her garbage bag diaper.

"Muh, member, how I was when I get um, mad at you, beb," she said, her hands up by her chest, shaking.

Spider-Man laughed and clapped his hands together. "Man, any time I bring another bitch back here, I always gotta make sure I do Janet first. Otherwise she'a kill me. She'a whoop my *ass*!"

Janet was smiling, staring up in different directions.

Spider-Man said, "She'a whoop my ass bro, come on!"

I laughed, feeling happy to be alive for three seconds.

Janet said, "Ey, um, beb, can you peez help me so I can go to the poath office peez?"

Spider-Man helped her into her wheelchair.

Her diaper made a swishing sound when she sat.

He took off her hat, straightened her hair, and put the hat back on.

She pointed at her lips.

Spider-Man kissed her.

She pointed down towards her crotch and said, "Gimme, a, a double. Hehe, shit."

Spider-Man looked at me and made a face. "You gotta be kiddin me!"

Janet laughed. "Shit. Bye, bebby."

She drove off in her wheelchair—out of the alley and onto the sidewalk—going towards the post office with a cup in her lap.

Spider-Man said, "Oh shit, look at this shit, man."

He took out a cellphone from his pocket and started scrolling.

He licked snot off his nose.

"Hol on, hol on," he said, moving his thumb sideways.

I took another pull off my tallboy.

"Bam, there it is," he said. "Nang!"

He came over and showed me his cellphone screen.

"Your phone is nicer than mine," I said.

"Check it out. I chat with this bitch like every week on the internet."

He showed me a picture of a woman with insanely big tits.

"They're double Z's," he said, wiping his nose. "Biggest in the world, man, gah be kiddin me. They're filled with air, bro. I talk to her once a week online. She from Vegas."

He scrolled through women, a big white loop of snot hanging from his nose and lip.

There were women with names like: BB Guns, Tiffany Towers, Pandora Peaks.

"Man, I saw Pandora Peaks at a bar," Spider-Man said, shaking his head. "I'm in Vegas. I'm at the bar. I turn around.

She's coming up to the bar for a drink. I said, 'You'rrrre Pandora Peaks right?' She like, 'Uh yep!' Man, she hugged me, and I's pressed up against her. Man, I fell to my knees."

"Shit," I said. "Fuckin bananas."

He laughed. "Fell to my *knees* bro," he said, holding up his hand.

"What does she do? Is she a stripper?"

"Nah, she just hangs out at bars, makes appearances, has a website. Some of the girls do porn. Tiffany Towers does porn, but she just sucks cock and eats pussy."

"You can do that?"

"Yeah," he said, "No uh, no intercourse."

"This chair is comfortable. What is this, bamboo?"

"Dahhhhhhhh. Fuckatta here."

Then this guy walked up from the other end of the alley.

He was wearing baggy jean shorts, a college football jersey, and a backwards baseball hat.

He had a long chin-beard.

Spider-Man said, "Ey, whattup DJ."

"Whattup whattup," DJ said.

He slapped hands with Spider-Man then me.

He sat on a parking block and took out a straightedge razor.

"Good morning to everyone," he said, touching the blade with his thumb. "Just woke up. Fucking slept at the park. How's everyone doing?"

He started shaving his cheeks a little, pinching the blade on either side to wipe off hair.

He shaved parts of his face, arms, and legs while we sat there drinking.

Any time a train would go over us, DJ would look up and point one or both of his middle fingers at the tracks.

He told me about how he worked at a church nearby, making temporary IDs for people.

"Oh yeah," he said, reaching into his pocket. He took out his wallet and handed some temporary IDs to Spider-Man. "There you go, girl."

Spider-Man checked them. "Dahhhhhhh, ey good-lookin!" he said, passing me one.

It had a black and white picture of his head.

It said, 'Janiya D— Jr.'

He put the IDs in his pocket. "Man, when I went to get these shits made, I fuckin walk in and they playin a movie in the sitting area. And what movie was it they playin? *Spider-Man*. Wooooo!"

DJ folded up his wallet and put it in his pocket. "Hell yeah, man."

Spider-Man said, "Man. I always cry watching that motherfucker. *Always*."

"At the end or something?" DJ said, wiping hair off his blade.

"At the whole thing!" Spider-Man said. "Hayo yeah, man."

He went over almost the entire storyline of the movie, using the sound effect 'Zshoo' a lot.

He was running all over the alley, getting exploded out of things.

The Happiness Inc. guy stood up and untucked his T-shirt from beneath his breasts, holding his stickers in the other hand.

His body odor was worse than mine in a way that made me want to worship him.

"You gonna put those up, man?" I said.

"Yeah," he said, looking at the stickers. "If there's anywhere fuggin dumb-ath Weed Wolf didn't yet. Jeez."

Weed Wolf was a guy who wrote 'Weed Wolf' on post office stickers then put them up everywhere.

"Man," DJ said, holding his razor out. "If I ever see Weed Wolf"—he held the blade a few inches from his face, moved it around over his eyes and nose and mouth and cheeks—"I got a buck fifty for em. Hundred fifty stitches to the face."

He smiled at me.

Spider-Man said, "Dahhh, plastic surgery, bro. Wha's really goin on!?"

"Hell yeah," DJ said. "Buck fifty for the bitches."

Spider-Man talked about this biker gang a mile west and how

they cut an X onto a dude's face if the dude was a pedophile or rapist or possibly neither.

A drop of water fell from the train tracks and put out his cigarette.

Perfect shot.

He checked the cigarette, put it behind his ear.

"But nah, them biker dude's baaaaaad motherfuckers, man. Gah be kiddin me. They don't use guns. They use knives, bricks, bats, tire irons, crow bars, wrenches. Don't fuck with them. That's nuts. Fuckin bananas."

DJ said, "Yeah, if you're a Chester the Molester, them dudes will fuck up your life. You're done."

He told a vague story occurring a few years earlier where a body was found in the area, throat cut open and stuffed with a severed dick.

Then he paused, took a deep breath, and pinched hair off his razor. "Ok, I have to go to work."

He pocketed his blade and walked away under the train tracks.

A train passed overhead and he held up both middle fingers.

Spider-Man and I finished our beers.

He looked down at his Air Force shirt and said, "Hayo yeah."

He showed me the other clothes in the bag—getting out each shirt to hold it up against himself then turn his head to the side and angle it up, blinking twice.

I referred to each shirt as, "Marvelous," "Fantastic," or "Exquisite."

And they were.

RED JELLY

I saw Janet out front of the post office today.
    She had a cup in her lap, collecting money.
    I asked her if she wanted something to eat.
    She said, "Um, jes, peez."
    "What do you want?"
    "Um, anything is ok peez."
    "What do you want? I'll go get it."
    "Um, I think, so-thing sweet."
    "Like what?" I said.
    "Um, gum?"
    "Gum?"
    "Jes peez."
    "What about food?"
    She smiled and started laughing.
    Her head bobbed up and down from a slouched position.
    "Ok, um, a burrito peez," she said.
    I went down the block and bought her a burrito.
    I dropped it off with her and offered to push her back to the alley but she said she'd be there later.

In the alley, Spider-Man was sitting on an overturned bucket and drinking a tallboy of coconut-flavored malt liquor.

He took out a pack of Dark Horse brand cigarettes and lit the last one.

I got out the bamboo chair and sat in it and told him it only felt like 80% bamboo.

"What, fuckatta here," he said, ashing into his empty pack.

He gave me a brief price history of Dark Horse cigarettes, including various places to buy them, the cheapest of which was at the California Blue Line stop—which then segued into a story about when he got arrested there.

"Man," he said. "Du, I's fucked up. I's dressing like Spider-Man and riding on top of the train. I thought I's Spider-Man. *The* Spider-Man."

"What?"

"Gah be kiddin me bro!" he said, smiling. He listed on his fingers. "I wore the white shoes, blue sweatpants, red tanktop, and a Spider-Man mask. From the Damen stop to the California stop. What!?"

I was laughing. "How did you not die?"

"Nah it's easy bro," he said. "You go in between cars and grab the handle and hop up—bwoop—gotta be kiddin me. You have to lay down though. And get off before that shit go underground. But nah man, that shit was awesome. I'd get myself a beer, leave it behind a bench, then ride on top of the train a couple stops, get off, grab another beer. Shit man, I'd slap hands with little kids at stops and whatnot. They thought I's Spider-Man." He ashed his cigarette. "But yeah, one time when I got off the cops were there and they arrested me and locked me up in the hospital, haha."

A train slowed down and came to a stop right above us.

Spider-Man stood up quick.

He grabbed my shirt and said, "Get up."

We moved.

He pointed at two oil stains on the ground by where we were sitting, fresh drops.

"At shit'll burn you," he said.

He laughed and held up both hands, curling his fingers and dragging them down his face while looking straight up so his eyes were mostly white.

In an extra-raspy voice, he said, "Guhhhh…no…my face! Burning from the oil…guhh."

He knelt down, reaching up, then quickly turned around, still kneeling.

He spun his head to make eye contact with me, covering the rest of his face in the inside of his elbow.

"Don't come near me," he said. "I've—changed." He did deep breaths that sounded like "Sersh…sersh…sersh." He yelled, "I said *get away*!"

"I can help!" I yelled, holding out my hand.

He stood up, laughing.

"That's my shit, man," he said. "Gah be nuts. Fuckatta here."

He grabbed his tallboy and took a big pull and sat back down on an overturned bucket.

This other guy I'd met at Danny's—Face—he walked up from the other end of the alley holding a 40.

"Wha's good, Janny?" Face said, clapping hands with Spider-Man.

Spider-Man said, "Ey man."

Face and I clapped hands and patted shoulders.

"Face," I said.

"Where I recognize you from, cous?" he said.

"Danny's."

"Aw shit, that's right, cous."

We sat down.

I gave Face the bamboo chair and I sat on an overturned bucket.

Spider-Man got a call on his phone.

It was Janet calling from the post office.

Her wheelchair wasn't working.

Spider-Man went to go help.

"Smash this bitch with me, cous," Face said, opening the 40.

I took a pull.

Face got out a Ziplock bag with some cigarettes he'd bought at the park.

"Now, I'm telling you, jo," he said. "At least two of these mine. Don't care what Janny say. Feel me?"

"Yeah."

"Yizzir," he said, lighting one, snapping the bag closed.

He had really long fingernails, tattoos on his hands.

I handed him the 40.

He took a huge pull.

"Man jo, don't wanna go to fuckin work tonight," he said, yawning, then shaking his head.

He talked about working at the Two Door.

Told me about one night after the bar closed. He and some of the other workers were in the alley drinking, and the brother of one of the bartenders called him a nigger.

"That foo always at the bar tryna fuck with me. So when he called me a nigger—I mean, that shit just a word jo, feel me?—but he trynna disrespect me in front of people. So I beat his ass, cous."

"Hell yeah."

Face laughed. "Du's brother was there too—he just watched, hah. Yizzir. He kept telling his brother to shut the fuck up but he wouldn't, so I beat his ass. Scraped his face along the alley and pushed his face into a puddle and shit. Don't be pushing my buttons, cous. I'm the coolest guy ever, but don't be pushing my buttons. Don't fuck with me, cous. I done kicked everyone's ass on this block."

He did a weird punch combination that looked like someone had wrapped him up in rubberbands and he was trying to get out.

He nodded towards Spider-Man's bed and said, "I done kicked Janny's ass too. He a bitch sometimes."

"Spider-Man?" I said.

"Yizzir. That nigga bi-polar. He flip out and I gotta beat the brakes off his ass." He laughed like 'Hik'ik'ik.' He sniffed and hawked on the ground. "Plus that nigga annoying, jo. Talkin bout, you mention anything about them comic books, nigga go on and tell you the whole damn movie. S'like, 'I thought I saw this shit, but oh well.'"

We both laughed.

Spider-Man came back into the alley, pushing Janet in her wheelchair.

He was sweating

He came up to Face. "Ey, you get those squares?"

Face cleared his throat. "Yeah, Janny."

He showed Spider-Man the ziplock bag of cigarettes.

They disagreed about how many were for who—with Face claiming to have paid for at least one, and Spider-Man maintaining that none were for Face.

Spider-Man started yelling, grabbed the bag. Then he said, "Nah fuck it, you know what, here, take your fucking cigarettes"—throwing the bag at Face.

Face tried to give the cigarettes back. "Come on, Janny. Relax, man."

Spider-Man took the bag of cigarettes and put one behind his ear, pocketing the rest, staring at Face.

Janet said, "Beb, um, can you fiss my foot peez?"

Spider-Man put her foot back into the plastic holder on her wheelchair.

She told Spider-Man about the burrito in the harness underneath her chair.

They split it.

He helped feed her while combing her hair.

A small piece of steak stuck to her nose after a bite.

She started to tell me about her online business with the piece of steak stuck to her nose.

She made bead necklaces and sold them online.

"Yo," Spider-Man said. He put the comb in his armpit, holding half the burrito in his hand. He pulled his collar down, showed me a necklace with alternating red and green plastic beads. "Shit's beautiful ain it?"

"Oh nice," I said. "Christmas style."

He said, "Dahhhh"—continuing to comb Janet's hair. "This my baby, I love my baby." He knelt by Janet and looked her in the eyes. "I'd do anything for you. You're my heart. I'd go to the gates of hell for you—go inside and close the gates to keep you out. I'd fight the Cerberus." He held up the burrito for Janet to bite. "Fuckin, kick the Sears Tower up into the air and lay in the street for it to land antenna-down on my chest. Anything."

"Hey man," I said to Face. "You hungry? I'm going to get some tacos."

"For certain, cous," he said.

I went and bought some tacos.

When I got back we all sat there in the alley under the train tracks, eating.

Janet mentioned she was learning to crochet at the library.

Spider-Man started to tell a story about his mother teaching his last woman to crochet but Janet interrupted.

"Wuh, who was that, huh?" she said. She turned to me. "See? Thuh, that's how I find out bout this shit. Fock."

Spider-Man threw down the comb. "My fucking ex-wife goddamnit! Tryna tell a story about my mom and you fuckin interrupt me. *Fuck you!*"

He crouched over her, his mouth right by her eyes.

She didn't say anything, staring up in different directions—her hands by her chest with the fingers out, piece of steak on the tip of her nose.

Everyone was quiet while Spider-Man screamed at her.

"You make me look bad in front of my *fuckin friends*," he yelled.

He grabbed Face's 40 off the ground and walked away, foam coming out of the 40 as he uncapped it.

Janet said, "He just um—he just need to, wuh, walk around."

Nobody said anything.

Face and I ate.

Spider-Man came back after a few minutes.

He sat down on a parking block and took a pull off the 40, pumping his one leg up and down on tiptoe.

He spoke quietly, one hand splayed out.

He told Janet not to interrupt him.

"When I talk about my mom, let me talk. Ok?"

She said ok.

He put the 40 down and hugged Janet. "Ok. I love you."

She said, "Luh, luff you more."

"Love you super most."

"I luff you, uh-finity."

"You're supposed to say I love you more than the galaxy," he said, smiling and blinking his eyes cartoonishly.

Then he grabbed Janet's nose between his first and middle finger and pulled his hand back with his thumb sticking out between the fingers. "Got your nose."

She grabbed his nose but didn't put her thumb through her fingers like you're supposed to.

They both laughed, holding each other's noses.

Eventually, he put her nose on his face and she put his on hers.

And I remembered the gum I had with me.

It was this shredded bubblegum, manufactured to look like chewing tobacco.

I'd bought a three pack a while ago—Ground Ball Grape, Swinging Sour Apple, and You'rrrrrrrrre Out! Original.

"You guys want some of this?" I said, reaching into my back pocket.

I'd been pretty liberal about offering people 'a pinch' wherever I went.

Because fuck yeah I wanted the pinches to go around.

Wanted everyone to know they could always rely on me to get a pinch.

The package I had with me was 'Ground Ball Grape' flavor.

It said, "Whole lotta gum inside!" on the front, below a cartoon baseball player holding a bat and looking ready to swing.

I handed the package to Spider-Man.

"Get yourself a pinch, man," I said.

He took a good-sized pinch.

"That's what I like to see," I said.

Spider-Man put the gum in his mouth and started chewing, rolling his eyes in circles and going, "Na, na, na."

Face laughed like 'Hik'ik'ik' and said, "Janny talking bout that na na na."

Pretty soon everyone had taken a pinch and was just enjoying everything.

We finished the 40.

Face left for work.

Spider-Man opened a dumpster by his bed and searched through it and got out a chessboard and a bag with the pieces.

We played chess while Janet continued work on a black and white beaded necklace.

We set the board on an overturned bucket and I used a bottlecap in place of a missing knight.

The game progressed slowly at first.

But then Spider-Man easily took a few of my pieces and put me in checkmate.

I acknowledged it by saying, "You motherfucker."

We reviewed all my possible moves and how each led to check.

I'd point out a move and Spider-Man would show how one of his pieces could attack, making the sound, 'Kersh.'

I shook his hand and helped him clean up the pieces.

We put the pieces and board back in the dumpster.

The dumpster was full of stuff—shirts, plastic containers, an umbrella, a package of cookies, etc.

I said, "Oh man, you got cookies?"

"Dahhhh, cookies. Gah be nuts. Here."

He handed me the package.

The cookies had a drop of red jelly in the middle, according to the front of the package.

"Thanks man," I said.

I hugged Janet goodbye and walked down the alley.
I ate the cookies on my way home.
The drop of red jelly was the best part.

FUNG BUSSY

Tonight when I passed by the alley no one was there, just a rat walking over Spider-Man's bed in the moonlight.

So I walked towards the Two Door.

Saw Face coming back from a liquor store down the block.

He had a 40 and a stack of fastfood cups.

He asked what I was doing. "We finna smash this 40 over by the bus stop, cous, come on."

At the bus stop there was a short fat guy, balding with a ponytail, wearing a huge Bears hoodie.

"Wha's good, Mike," Face said, slapping hands with him.

Mike was talking to a guy slumped over on the bus stop bench.

"Speedy," Mike said. "I'm fucking telling you."

Face pointed at the guy on the bus stop bench and said, "This my dude, Speedy. He coo man, but he fucked up tonight. Yizzir."

Speedy was a skinny old man wearing an Army coat, sitting on the bus stop bench with his limp legs and a walking cane.

I sat down next to him.

He had a tiny ponytail tied with a broken rubberband.

Face poured out the 40 into fastfood cups and handed everyone a cup.

"Speedy," I said, smiling at Speedy.

He laughed like, 'Nehehe' with a smile that slowly formed after he started laughing.

Then he started talking to me.

Drunk as fuck, just mumbling shit.

Something about Vietnam.

Something about being on the ground.

Something about running through bullets.

Something about motherfuckers.

Something about the Air Force.

I could only understand 1/3 of what he was saying.

Most of it sounded like, "Fussuh buminna...."

I'd just stare at him and when he stopped every once in a while, I'd say, "Yep."

And he'd say, "N'yep" then start again with the "bussa ummina...."

The Blue Line train passed on a bridge over Fullerton.

Speedy made a gun with his hand and pointed it at the train and moved his hand up and down, his mouth moving.

When the train cleared I could hear him going, "Pish pish pish" for each shot.

"Man, Air Force shit is pussy shit," he said. "Air Force is ambush...flying...bombs. Pussy shit."

He kept pronouncing 'pussy' like 'bussy.'

"Air Force is for bussy shit," he said, snot going into his mouth.

Then something about Vietnam again.

Something about bullets.

He leaned forward and rolled up a pant leg, showing me the bullet scars on his calf.

"Z?" he said.

He almost fell forward but I grabbed him.

He tried to spit but it landed all over him.

Mike was pacing—cigarette in one hand, other hand in pocket—smiling at me and Speedy.

He went up to Face and said, "So hey man, I think I'm gonna copy some pornos and sell em out here. Do like, 2 for 10 or something."

Face said, "O'boy down the block already do that shit, but he do 3 for 10."

"Really?" Mike said.

"Yizzir."

"Fuck," Mike said. He started pacing again. He smiled at me and said, "Fuck"—widening his eyes a little.

Face said, "Ey but for real, we gotta get Speedy dumb-ass a cab, man. He my pops, but he out here all fucked up and he needa get home. I'ont wanna leave him out here when I clean up in this bitch."

Face and Mike vaguely waved to cabs down the block across the street, opposite corner.

I sat there drinking my beer.

There were no cabs on our street.

"I got money," Speedy told me. He was trying to reach into his pockets. "25 dollars an hour," he kept saying. "I make money."

Every once in a while he'd laugh like, 'Nehehehe'—with a smile that slowly formed after he started laughing.

With that snake-like wrinkly face.

And that one big tooth in front.

"Doe fuck Korean girls," Speedy said. "Watch out, they gah [something something] in the bussy, nehe."

Face said, "Speedy, where you finna stay tonight? You my pops, but you done tonight, and I got work, so—"

"Stayin at yer place, bussy. Take me'a your place."

Face said, "Uh uh, fuck that. I'ont need you. You ain got no cootie cat." He gestured by his crotch. "Sorry padna, but you ain got no split."

Speedy said, "Ey, fuck you marfucker, nehehe."

I laughed too.

Face put his hands in a prayer gesture. "Speedy, please, shut the fuck up, man. I'm trynna help you and you pissin me off, jo."

Speedy said some shit that no one understood, wiping off his bottom lip slowly with his knuckle.

It looked like he was waiting for our response, but no one said anything.

Then, louder, he said, "Bussy. I'nt some bussy!"

He had his mouth open a little, tongue along his bottom lip. And that little wormy vein on his temple.

"I'na fuck a bish," he said.

Face laughed like 'Hik'ik'ik' and slapped Mike's arm.

Mike was taking a drag of his cigarette—fingers still around it—shaking his head no with his eyes closed.

"I'na fuck a bish," Speedy said. "Some bussy."

On the inside of the bus stop shelter, there was an ad for the Lincoln Park Zoo.

The ad showed stingrays in light-blue water.

Mike pointed at the ad and said, "Ey Speedy, you can fuck one of those."

Speedy was nodding off, chin against his chest and hiccupping at intervals.

I caught him before he fell, resting him against the glass of the bus stop shelter.

Face said, "Come on, man. We gettin you home. Wake the fuck up."

Speedy opened his eyes, a confused look on his face.

Face and I had to pick him up and bring him to the closest main street to hail a cab.

We each grabbed one of Speedy's arms and put it around our shoulders, taking a leg underneath the thigh.

I got some spit on my neck from Speedy's coat and his jeans were all pissed and steamy.

Oh Speedy.

Face and I carried him to a bench on Milwaukee Ave. and sat him down.

We hailed a cab.

A cab stopped.

It was a van.

Face and I lifted Speedy inside.

Cabby said, "No. Can't do. Can't do this, man."

Face said, "Come on, man. His wife or son or somebody will be waiting for him. Just take him home."

Cabby said, "Wife and son? No. No, man."

I said I'd go with.

Face said, "Nah man" then turned to the cabby again. "Come on, man. Just drive him home. He know his address and shit. S'all good."

Cabby said, "Can't do that, man. No no."

"I'll go with, man," I said.

Cabby looked at me and said, "Yes, you go with. Is ok."

Face didn't say anything for a second. Then he shrugged. "Aight jo, I'm sorry. Come find me when you back around. Come find me at the bar."

I slapped hands with him and got in the cab.

The cab smelled like piss and old rain.

Speedy mumbled about money, trying to put his hands in his pants pockets.

Something about 900 dollars on him.

Something about paying for my way back.

Something something.

Bussy.

Speedy gave the cabby an address and we drove toward it.

The cabby started to apologize.

Said he didn't know.

Said he didn't want to have to carry him, couldn't carry him.

"Can't do this, my man, you know?" he said, making eye contact with me in the rearview mirror at a stoplight.

"Yeah, no problem," I said.

Speedy tapped my arm and loudly whispered, "Heece a bussy"—then hiccupped.

I laughed.

The cabby laughed making eye contact again in the rearview mirror.

He turned up the contemporary dance music on the radio and raised his eyebrows to me in the rearview mirror. "I make it louder?"

"Hell yeah," I said, looking out the window.

And we drove.

Speedy tapped my arm with his hand.

He nodded toward the cabby and said, "S'a bussy"—then fell sideways a little.

I caught him and straightened him as the contemporary dance music played.

Cabby said, "I turn here? Here good?"

Speedy said, "No, kip goin. Go a my house, marfucker. I get paid, I have a lot of money. I make more'n you."

Cabby turned down the music. "Yes ok, that's good my friend. Ok."

Speedy took out a handful of crumpled money and showed me.

I opened my eyes real big. "Whoa, nice."

Speedy laughed, resting against the door and holding the money out.

I laughed.

That made Speedy laugh more.

The cabby was making eye contact with me in the rearview mirror.

He started laughing too.

It was chaos.

When we got to Speedy's place there was no wife or son out front!

Just a small house with a gate and staircase and some signs about not having a dog on the premises.

"Pull up here, pull up here," Speedy said, pointing to a utility van out front his house. "Don't hit my van, it has a security system, ya fung bussy."

I laughed.

Every time I laughed, Speedy'd laugh and look at me.

Felt like we were both 8 years old, at a sleepover.

Speedy told the cabby to back into the alley a little to line up his door with the sidewalk. "Pull up, pull up," he kept saying.

Cabby kept saying, "Yes yes, pay here, pay here."

Speedy handed the cabby a handful of bills.

He offered to pay for my ride back but I said I'd walk, lying about how I knew some people who lived nearby—the old "I know people" routine.

Oh brother!!!

The cabby got out and opened the door for us then stood back while I got Speedy out myself.

I almost dropped him at first because my arms weren't securely around him, all the weight on my fingers and wrists.

But then I adjusted.

"Put me onna steps," he said, looking over my shoulder at his house.

I carried him down the cab's ramp and onto the sidewalk.

Looking at the cabby over my shoulder, he said, "Heece a bussy anway."

I laughed.

The cabby laughed. "Is ok?"

I said yeah.

He got in his cab and drove away.

I carried Speedy up the front steps, set him down so he had space to lean back.

"Anks," he said. "I'n sit here and smoke a square. Shh, I mean a joint, nehe."

I laughed and nodded, said goodbye.

He said, "Ok, I see you Friday," and fell asleep on the stairs.

It was a really long walk back.

There was already a blister covering my entire left heel, from not wearing socks with my boots.

The blister came off the heel immediately, squishing with each step.

The fucking squishes.

Lord Almighty, the fucking squishes.

Up above, the moonlit clouds looked rippled, like the ribcage of some giant thing digesting me.

And I wondered if the direction I was going went down into the digestive system or up out of it.

Wondered what difference it made.

There was a bug hovering over a small pool of ice cream on the sidewalk.

Like a firefly, but it wasn't a firefly.

And I could've stepped on it and killed it.

But I didn't.

Be thankful, little bug.

For in my world, you are just a little bug.

IN MY CASTLE/
FUCK THE WORLD

I passed by Spider-Man's alley this afternoon and saw Face pissing on a dumpster.

"Whattup cous?" he said, zipping up.

He started walking down the alley and motioned for me to follow.

Spider-Man and Janet still weren't there, but there were two other guys—Larry and Craig—sharing a 40.

Larry was sitting on an overturned bucket.

I shook hands with him and sat on a parking block.

He smiled, clasping his hands between his knees.

He was overweight, wearing this big stretched-out T-shirt.

"Hoowee, namn," he said.

Craig sat on the ground with his back against a column of the train tracks, holding a crackpipe and a lighter.

He had no shirt on, baggy jeans tied off with a belt, and unlaced peanut-butter-colored work boots—eyes hyped and yellow.

He said, "Hey, we uh, doing some choice activities here."

Face said, "Don't worry. This cat coo as shit."

I said hi.

Craig looked at me for a second.

Then he smiled, holding out his hand.

"Craig Williams," he said.

I thought it'd be funny to kiss his hand and say, "Nice to meet you."

But instead we shook hands and locked thumbs.

"Craig Williams," he said again. "Thass British, but I'm talkin bout I'm become Chinese to my kids if I stay out here too long. Talkin bout 'One Gone Too Long.'"

He took a huge hit off the crackpipe, turning it slow and watching with his eyes crossed.

He exhaled.

"Yizzir," Face said, then cleared his throat.

"Hoowee, namn," Larry said, his hands still clasped between his knees.

Another guy came walking down the alley.

Troy.

I'd seen him around but never really talked to him because he was always too drunk to remember me.

He came up and said, "Ey, hassa goin erybody?"

Skinny, sunburned, and bald.

He wore an oversized white tanktop and long wide-legged shorts with the brand name 'spraypainted' on one of the legs.

There was a foam flower behind his ear.

Face said, "Nice petunia, Petunia."

Troy said, "Anks"—poking through a handful of cigarette butts he'd collected.

His hands were gray and dry like elephant skin, bleeding through cracks.

"Troy, fuck you been?" Craig said, holding up his hands. "You get that ice?"

"Huh?" Troy said. "I's?"

"Yeah, you suppose'a get ice. I gave you that dollar before. We tryna ice this beer, man."

Troy barked through some mucus. "Nah man, I never got any dollar."

Craig laughed. "What? Man, bullshit you didn't."

He started to stand up.

Troy just shook his head and said, "Hol on, be right back"—holding the petunia in place with one hand, cigarette butts with the other as he walked away.

There was a strip of hair along his neck where he'd missed shaving.

Troy.

"Man, fuck that motherfucker," Craig said, resting back against the brick wall behind him, looking at the crackpipe.

He touched an area on his ribs, lightly scratching.

He lifted his arm and pinched the area a little, showed me some scarring on his ribcage.

"Man," Craig said, smiling. "This shit from this one bitch I used to date, Suzie. Bitch was Canadian, Spanish, and something else. You member her, Face? Face, I done told you this story."

Face was staring at the ground. He looked up and said, "Huh? Nah man."

Craig said, "Yeah jo, Suzie—when she, you know."

He waited for Face to respond.

When Face didn't respond, Craig turned to me and said, "Bitch lit me on fire while I's sleeping."

"Oh shit," I said, trying not to smile.

But then Craig smiled, so whatever.

"So it's like this," he said, licking his lips. "Man, one time she thought she caught me cheatin, and she locked herself in the bathroom. I's poundin, yelling, 'Let me in let me in.' She kept saying, 'One second, one second.' So I broke open the door and she in the bathtub cuttin her arm up with a motherfuckin razor. I told her, 'Baby, I'm not cheatin.' I told her, I said baby, get mad at the person cheating when that happens. Then shit, one night I pass out drunk, ok. And she found a number and a name in my pants pocket. Calls the bitch up. My ass wake up to something cold and wet. She pouring rubbing alcohol on me. She talkin bout, 'You said hurt the person cheating on you, not yourself.' So she lit my ass on fire, jo. And my dumbass, hah, instead of rolling around, I run to the bathroom. Got my dumbass burnt. Second-degree burns, jo."

Face was laughing like 'Hik'ik'ik'—his shoulders going up and down.

Larry said, "Hoowee, namn."

He'd mostly been sitting there with his hands clasped between his knees, saying, "Hoowee, namn" and sometimes grabbing at the small floating things blowing off nearby trees.

A butterfly flew by.

Face turned to Craig and backhanded him on the chest. "Ey, you see that butterfly, cous?"

Craig said, "Yeah, uh huh, that orange one. What's that? It's a—"

"A monarch," Face said.

"Yeah, monarch," Craig said. He clicked his teeth. "Man, look at you, Bug Man."

"Yizzir," Face said.

Craig laughed, kept licking his lips.

His lips were like, white with dryness.

Me, I was trying to get crust out of my eye.

Things were happening so fast.

Worlds of possibility crumbled into newer and larger worlds so fast, it was as if none existed.

Craig said he had a riddle for me. "Alright, this a real brainteaser," he said, sitting up a little. His hand looked like he was about to karate chop something. "Alright, you got two coins. They equal 30 cents. One is NOT a quarter." He folded his hands. "What are they?"

I thought.

"One is a quarter and one is a nickel," I said.

He clicked his teeth. "Dag, jo."

It was the first riddle I'd ever solved.

Larry said, "Hoowee, namn."

Face laughed like, 'Hik'ik'ik.'

He took a cigarette butt from behind his ear and lit it, offering Craig a pull.

Craig said, "Man, you know I done quit smoking. Come on, man, I'm allergic to cancer. Shit, I got stress too. My motherfuckin job got me travelling all over. I *should* be smoking like I kilt Jesus." His cellphone rang. He ignored it. "Work. Man, them dudes I work for, they be I-talian and shit. Talkin bout, 'Ey paisan! Goomba! Yo, ey!' Them motherfuckers, they all live up in Norwood Park and shit. Up northwest. They own *everything*, man. They got that strip place called The Pink Monkey. They told me I could work the door and shit but I said nah. Not with them girls there, jo. Haha. I'm a hound dog, man. Plus I'd be selling powder to they asses in no time. Powder powder *powder*. Who wannit?"

Face laughed. "You feel me, cous?"

"Them girls love they powder," Craig said. "You want the best powder, go to them girls." He pointed at the ground beside me. "Shit, you snort gravel, they get the best gravel."

I laughed.

Snorting gravel up into my brain where it ricochets at an increasing speed until becoming a humming sound, completely liquefying my entire head, which then spills down over my body in a perfect coating.

Larry coughed. "Hoowee. Namn."

He picked up the 40 off the ground and took a pull, holding the neck with one hand and the bottom with the other.

"Pass the pain," Craig said, sitting up.

He tipped his hat back and scratched his head, took the 40 from Larry.

A train passed above us.

After it passed, Face looked at me. "Ey, how come I ain see you the other night."

I pushed one nostril closed and blew a hard booger out of the other nostril. "It was late when I got back from taking Speedy home."

"Oh yeah," he said, smiling. "Hik'ik'ik. Dang, cous. Ey, God gone bless you for that, though. F'sho. You the man. I got you. Even if I ain got shit, I still got you. Face got two dollars in his pocket then you got two dollars. And I'on't even have to say that, cous."

"Yeah man," I said.

Craig was idly tapping his crackpipe with the metal part of his lighter. "Let's play some cards or something," he said.

Face got a pack of cards from Spider-Man's dumpster and broke down a cardboard box, laying it on the ground.

We played spades, sharing a 40 Face had newly opened.

"Aw man, forgot," Craig said, shuffling the cards. "Scrappy done gave me this shit here. You seen this, Face?"

Craig went into his backpack and got out a small square calendar(?)/book(?) called *A Thousand Places to See Before You Die*.

He held it out for everyone, flipping through the pictures.

One was a castle on a small mountain.

"Shit," Craig said, smiling. "Tryna live in *this* bitch."

Larry looked at the castle, arranging his cards and chewing his bald gums. "H'only issue I'd be worried bout be how to git food up there. Specially when it snows. But hoowee, namn."

Craig was looking at the castle. "Man, if I lived there, I be like 'Fuck the world, I'm in my castle, jo, fuck *all* y'all.'"

It felt cooler out.

I noticed it was beginning to get dark.

And for a couple seconds, it was scary—like that meant the world was breaking, or expired, or bruised, or something worse.

It was really scary for a couple seconds but then I calmed down.

BED THRONE, PISS JUG, VICELORDS

Larry slept out front of the library.

On the way to the Two Door tonight I saw him in his sleepingbag, lying on his side.

He had his elbow against the ground, head propped up in hand.

I waved. "Larry, yo."

He waved and said, "Hooooo"—slowly standing up.

He wobbled, looking up into the air somewhere.

"Larry, how you doing?" I said, shaking his hand.

He said, "Man, I am FUH-TUP. I's at the Two Door watching the Howx game. Hoooo."

The Howx game.

Many play the Howx game and many lose.

"Hooo, I drank too much," he said. "Naaaaamn. What're you doin?"

"Nothing," I said.

"Namn. I am, FUH-TUP!"

"Walk with me back to the Two Door."

He said, "N'ok yeah," but then didn't move when I started walking.

He stood there, trying to balance.

"Hoowee, namn," he said, taking off his hat and rubbing his head.

I walked down the street towards the Two Door.

Face was at the bus stop out front, smoking a cigarette.

He was wearing a big Blackhawks 2010 Stanley Cup Champions T-shirt and a red White Sox hat backwards.

"Wha's good, cous?" he said, slapping my hand then pulling me in for a hug.

"Nothin, man."

"Shit, you wanna walk with me? I got some beers and a little bit of a fiff back at my mama crib. We can tip some with bitch-ass Troy if you wanna."

Troy lived in an alley near Face's mom's house, where Face stayed.

On the way there, we passed the library.

Larry was asleep.

"Hahhhh, he smack-drunk," Face said. "They threw his ass out after he ain have no money. Du at the bar didn't have to be so rough wit his ass but he ain have no money."

Oh Larry.

Larry Larry Larry.

We went into an alley behind a gas station.

Someone had written, 'One more chance' in thick-tipped permanent marker on a dumpster.

There were drips coming off the letters.

I imagined the drips coming from the sky—lowering from rain clouds—and everyone gets to pick one to climb—and when you get to the top you get something—but whatever you get, it's yours and there's nothing you can do about it.

Nothing!

Face and I passed backyards and gangways and dumpsters,

piles of garbage, a garage with a large gang tag that'd been x'd out and inverted in red.

A pit bull rushed up to the gate of a chainlink fence, barking at us.

It made sideways eye contact with me, going, 'Oorv, oorv.'

Part of me wanted to grab it by the head and kiss it right on the lips then let it eat my face off.

The other part of me wanted the exact same thing.

Troy's place was down the alley, by an old freight door—with a loading ramp held up by metal wire on each side, a throne of beds stacked on each other.

Face stood by a dumpster and tapped the lid with his fingernails. "Wha's good, T?"

Troy lay in bed with a stained hoodie on, coughing, his eyes barely open.

He was drunk as fuck, pasty spit around his mouth.

He opened his eyes a little. "Wah? Ey, hassa goin, man?"

He barked out some mucus.

"You sleepin?" Face said, lighting half a cigarette.

Troy said, "Nah, I mean, issa trissa but, heh. I mean, yeah, I's sleepin a lil haha." Then he leaned over. "Hol on a sec, there."

He grabbed a plastic jug near his bed and put it beneath his blankets, pissed.

He set the jug back down, almost knocking it over.

"Ohps," he said, catching the jug and settling it.

Face said, "Be right back. Finna get them beers."

He jogged down the alley.

I noticed there was a roof ten feet above Troy and his bed throne.

"Oh man, that's nice," I said. "Just saw that."

Troy gestured to it with his hand. "Aw yeah, tissa dissa thing, it's, I mean ey…the rain starts pouring, ey, RUN IT!"

"RUN IT!" was something he said a lot—like "Yes!" or "All right!"

I think it referred to using a credit card, like when you 'run it' through the sliding machine.

Or maybe it was football-related.

Not sure.

Troy's main sayings were:

"That's not my problem/That's on you/Run it!"

I leaned on a dumpster, my elbows and forearms on the lid.

Another beautiful day.

Glad to be alive and have friends.

Troy was already asleep again, both hands on his chest.

A rat crawled out from behind the freight door and onto his blanket.

He partially woke up, trying to launch/tent the rat off him by pushing his hands up under areas of the blanket.

On the third attempt, he launched the rat off the blanket.

Face came back with a 1/3-full fifth and an Old Style 12-pack containing different bottles of beer he'd taken from the Two Door.

He passed me the fifth and I took a pull, checked the bottle.

McCormick's whiskey.

Special Reserve.

Since 1856.

I took another pull.

The first pull tasted like whiskey and the second one tasted like something else—something you'd use as an extreme measure against acne.

I drank warm beer along with it, hoping to die in my sleep.

"Thanks man," I said to Face, holding up my Old Style.

"What I always tell you?" Face said.

I did an impression of him. "You good, cous? You need something?"

Face laughed, stomping the ground a little.

He switched his hat from back/left to straight backwards.

Troy pointed. "Whassa, ey, y'goin neutral there?"

Face smiled. "Yizzir."

Troy said, "Folkz and People and issa all that gang bullshit, heh."

Face flipped his hat to the right. "This for them Folkz." Then flipped it to the left. "This for People." He looked at me, nodded upwards. "Who you with, cous? Who you with?"

I said, "You know damn well I got Folk love, bitch, till the motherfuckin world blow."

Face laughed, slapping the dumpster lid.

"For certain, cous," he said. Then he cleared his throat and looked serious. "But nah, man. I done seen all that shit growing up in the projects. Yizzir, I done see some shit people never see in they goddamn *life,* man. Damn jo, sometimes I say to myself, 'Face, how you survive this shit? How you still here?'" He nodded a little, looking at me. "We talkin bout, 'Get Mine, Protect Yours,' cous. And them niggas is nasty."

He described the layout of the different buildings in the projects where he grew up.

It was where the Bulls and Blackhawks played, a mile and a half outside of The Loop.

"See, they was fo buildings in my projects. Different gang in each building, cous. They was um, GDs, BDs, Foes, and Travs. I's hustling Travs, cous."

"Travelling Vicelords," I said.

"Yizzir. Fo buildings. GDs in this one"—he motioned with his hand, keeping his other hand at a different location—"BDs right here, and Foes up in there, and us Travs, we's in this building."

He took a pull off the fifth and passed it.

I took a pull.

Face said, "We had a abandoned apartment at the bottom of my building." He pointed at the large freight door behind Troy's bed, where Troy was sleeping. "And in the middle, they was a big empty window. Talkin bout, we use'a creep up along against the wall, then"—he turned sideways and held out an imaginary gun—"Blaow Blaow. Poppin BDs all day." He put up a VL sign on his hand. He was smiling at me, shaking his head. "I use'a think I'd never die, cous. Use'a think I's fucking unstoppable. I use'a think them bullets"—he stuck his chest out then touched all his fingers to his chest, let his hands drop—"clink, clink, talkin bout them bullets just fall right off me, cous. That's what I thought. Ain shit you could do to me back then. But nah, then they kilt my friend—my nigga, Big Soft. That was my boy. Man jo, he a skinny ass motherfucker man, shit. Buck oh five with the rocks and Hennessy in his pants, cous. Crook-eyed motherfucker. But that nigga had the whole hood scared. Nobody in our building fucked with him, jo. Then, one night I's with him, and we's running from some hoods blassin at us, cause you know I done been shot at 19,000 times. And motherfuckers got him with a AK." He pointed to just above one hip, "Bullet went from here"—then pointed to his other hip—"all the way out here. I done seen him fall and die in the street. Fucked me up. That's when I got out of the bullshit, man."

"They didn't try to kill you?" I said.

"Hell nah. That's some bullshit. Ain no jump in jump out with us. No blood in/blood out. Uh uh. We ain do that bullshit, rabbit-ass gang shit. Nah. You don't put yo hands on me. That's for the Puerto Rican, fuckin, Messican gangs. Shit though, not the brothers. You don't put yo hands on the brothers. How I'm gonna help yo ass when you kickin me and shit? Fuck nah, nigga. Don't put yo hands on me."

Troy woke up a little, barking out some mucus.

Face said, "Oh sorry, T." He shook his head and clicked his teeth. "Nah but I done seen it all though, cous. Yizzir. I done see some shit," He put a finger to his temple. "I wish I had a plug or some shit, put my mind inside yo mind." He pointed to the scar on his cheek. "See this shit. Motherfuckers cut me over some rocks. Like fo lil rocks. Yizzir. I done seen motherfuckers shoot a nigga right in the face." He pointed a gun at his face and went, "Blahhhhh"—staggering back a little. "I done seen a nigga get his head cut off and thowed out a 15-story window. I done seen a motherfucker—you know them 2 by 4's?—I done see a motherfucker tied up with a arm on each end of a 2 by 4 and a motherfucker take a bat and bust up all this here"—pointing to his ribs. "Man, I had to run out, I was puking from hearing nothing but bones crackin. Cruck cruck cruck. I done seen a motherfucker thowed down the uh, you know them garbage chutes? Over some 20 dollars man, shit. That's how we did it though, cous. We use'a kick it and bang all the time. I'd have my rocks, my Hennessy, some rolls, fucking everything. Sit on the stoop with my strap." He lifted his shirt a little by his waistband. "Man, one time we was on the block and this nigga went through the alley with a, you know a, a tommy gun? Fucking bussin that shit for like three minutes straight. Big ass bulletholes in the metal mailbox in our building, jo. Could put yo thumb in the holes, man. But shit, I'on't know. I never gave a fuck bout that shit, cous. I thought I's the devil hisself sometimes. I eat a bullet like some fuckin mints." He speared out his gum with his long pinkynail and took a pull off the fifth then put the gum back in his mouth. "Oh shit, that remind me. Troy, you seen that motherfucker Jeffrey?"

Troy was asleep.

"Troy?" Face said. "Ey."

Troy opened his eyes and tried to focus.

"You seen Jeffrey?"

"Who?"

"Jeffrey," Face said, louder.

Troy wiped his eyes. "Oh yeah frissa bissa, haha, becussa the burrito thing?"

He rested his hands on his chest, fingers interlaced and seemingly revived from his nap.

"Yeah man, fuck that," Face said. "That nigga on some treason shit." He looked at me and said, "Man this du Jeffrey, he come up to me outside the bar, talkin bout, he need money for a burrito. Ok. So I gave him half. I gave him three dollars so he could get hisself a burrito. But I done tol him before he left—" Face clapped his hands together, then took one hand out and pointed at me, "I tol him: save me a little. I knew he was hungry so I didn't say no 'Save me half.' I said, you know, 'Just save me a little.'"

"Uh oh," I said.

Troy was already laughing/coughing a little.

Face clamped his teeth together. "That motherfucker ate the whole damn thing cept for a lil scrap a some lettuce."

Troy started laughing really hard. He wiped his eyes and said, "Issa bissa, ey, he fung kilt that thing, run it!"

Face said, "Next time I see him, I'ma whoop that nigga's *ass*, jo. Talkin bout, left me with a little scrap a some lettuce and shit—ain even any meat in it." Then he paused like he was alone, and in a really quiet voice he said, "Ey you know what though, god bless him. If he was hungry enough to smash that burrito like that, gobbling it down like that, then he needed it, cous. I got food at my mom crib, you know? It's aight." He shook his head, smiling. "He smashed it though. Suh-mashed that bitch."

Troy was laughing. "Kilt that fung thing."

He cleared some mucus with a little bark.

"God bless him then," Face said. He looked at me. "S'like how you did good for my man Speedy. God gon do you right by you f'that." He turned to Troy. "Ey, T. Thissa coo cat right here. He help Speedy dumb-ass out."

Face told him the story.

Troy laughed. "That marfucker. You know why his lecks don't fung work right?"

"He told me he was in Vietnam," I said. "And that the Air Force is for pussies."

Troy laughed/coughed.

Face laughed like, 'Hik'ik'ik' as he got out a cigarette, spearing gum out of his mouth with his pinky nail. "Nah man. Speedy a dumb motherfucker. Swear to god. I love that man, but he fucking dumb as it is, cous. That motherfucker used to be about that graffiti shit and whatnot, that taggin. And his dumbass started getting high off the spraypaint. You know, you uh, spray alla paint in a bag then breave it in. Dumb ass done fucked up his spinal cord."

Troy said, "Issa, uh, the, the"—pointing up into the air, "Huffing. Assa, yeah, called huffing."

"Yeah, huffing," Face said. He clicked his teeth, making an 'oh well' expression. "Yizzir."

I briefly imagined a withered root as Speedy's spinal cord.

Running it between my teeth to scrape off what little's left.

My only prayer being, "I'll always take what little's left."

"Scrap a some lettuce," I said, shrugging.

Face laughed. "Tellin you, that nigga suh*mashed* that bitch. Left jussa scrap a some lettuce and shit."

Troy laughed a little, half-asleep again.

He stretched out his arms and put them behind his head.

He accidentally hit the piss jug with his elbow and the jug wobbled, but he grabbed it and settled it.

Face said, "Ey, Troy, gimme that beer."

Troy grabbed the piss jug and said, "This beer?"

Face laughed.

Troy laughed, waving his hand down like 'nah just kidding.'

Then he grabbed a 40 by his bed and handed it to Face.

Face said, "What if I just take this shit from you right now, on some gangsta shit."

Troy said, "Go ahead, issa bissa, yo, look, I mean, fine. I don't give a fuck about the beer. Just don't take the piss ok?"

Face laughed, slapping the dumpster lid a little, holding the 40 up high.

Troy said, "Leave the apple juice, y'know? I need my vitamin C in the morning."

Face was stomping and laughing.

He took a big pull off the 40 and passed it to me.

This guy rode up on a mountain bike and came to a stop right in front of us with a small skid.

Couldn't even tell where he came from.

It was an older guy in an Army jacket.

He had long hair in a ponytail, a huge hook nose, handlebar moustache, no front or top/bottom teeth, baseball hat with a small flashlight taped to the bill.

I said hi to him and he started talking to me.

He had a light lisping voice with a seemingly Canadian accent.

He kept laughing like, 'Sis sis sis' then saying, "Hoo hoo."

His eyes slowly slanted inward and remained crossed for a few seconds.

"Hey man," he said. "Wanna know something? I mean, hey um, do you like videogame systems?"

"Yeah," I said.

"Which one do you have?"

"I don't have one."

He unzipped a bag attached to his bike. "Hey um, because, wanna know something? Guess what, there's this wireless controller I got for sale. Twinny dollars. Yeah."

He showed me a wireless controller, still in the box.

"Oh nice," I said.

"Yeah um, because, guess what. Wanna guess what? It's brand new. The assholes at the game store threw it out in the alley. You know what? I have to say this, and I'm sorry, but I like living in the city because of how wasteful people are. Yeah. Hoo hoo. Wanna know, um, no I mean how much you think this is?"

"Like, sixty dollars? Fifty dollars?"

"No. Forty-nine ninety-nine."

He put it back in the bag attached to his bike.

"I got all kinds of stuff," he said. "Hey um, you smoke weed?" He got out a little pipe and a grinder. "Hey how about this for something, want to know how much this grinder costed?"

"Thirty dollars."

"No. Nothing dollars. I got it for free when I worked security at this concert place. This stupid girl, oh man, hoo hoo, wanna know how stupid she was, man? She comes up to me and says, 'Hey I got those doses.' LSD. She said that to me, and I'm like, I pointed at the word 'Security' on my shirt. Thank you! I took her doses and this grinder."

Both his eyes went inward toward his nose for a few seconds.

Troy said, "Ey, don't smoke that over here. I don't want it smelling over here, I know all the neighbors. Come on."

Bike Guy and I walked ten feet away, around the corner a little.

I could hear Troy saying, "You know, come on. This my place. People have rules for their houses. I have rules for my place."

Bike Guy lit his pipe and took a pull and held it in, pinching his nose shut.

He laughed like "Sis sis sis" as he exhaled.

I took the remaining pull and thanked him.

He looked at me.

Both his eyes went inward.

He said, "If you know anyone who um, wants that controller, let me know, man."

"I will."

We went back around the corner.

Bike Guy walked over to his bike, reached into his coat, and took out a tallboy of Old Style from an inside pocket.

He put the tallboy into the waterbottle slot on his bike and rode away.

"You guys know him?" I said.

Face said, "Yeah he come around here once a while. That du fucking weird, cous."

Troy said, "Ey, not my problem," half-asleep. Then he woke up and looked around a little. "Ey, hassa goin?"

Face told a story about how he'd been drinking here at Troy's one night, with one other guy, and the Bike Guy came up and talked to them.

"So this crook-eye bike du talkin us. Me and o'boy sitting side by side over here. And o'boy say, 'Who is you talkin to, me or him?'"

Face and Troy started laughing hard.

I laughed.

Oh man.

"Who is you talkin to," Face said again, in a breathless/highpitched voice, pointing from eye to eye.

Troy looked at me and said, "Hey man, wait till you hear the rest"—putting the piss jug back under the blankets.

Face said, "When the motherfucker rode down toward the street, o'boy like, 'Make sure you look boaf ways!'"

He and Troy started laughing again.

Troy coughed like 'kunk kunk.'

Face slid down the dumpster a little as he pounded the top of it.

"Boaf ways," he said, kneeling behind the dumpster laughing. "Hahhhhh."

I was smiling.

It was a nice night

The perfect night to die in your sleep.

I said, "Have either of you guys seen Spider-Man? I haven't seen him in a while."

Face took a pull off the fifth and ate the gum back off his nail. "Yeah where Janny at? He supposed to be back already."

Troy said, "Bissa no, I mean heece back around. He got kicked out of that, assissa, assisted living place with Janet, y'know? S'all bullshit, man. He uses her. But ey, whatever. Not my problem."

Face said, "Yeah, he a bastard. Beatin on her and shit."

"Ey, lissa," Troy said. "He has her sit out front the fung post office all day. She makes six'y dollars in one day. She gives it all to him. His lazy ass goes out and drinks while she sits out front in her fung wheelchair."

"Yeah he an assho," Face said, nodding, clearing his throat. "I seenem slap her around too."

"But ey, not my problem," Troy said.

Face took a pull off the fifth. "Hey, you know what I noticed T? Shit's always about you, man. No matter what we talkin bout. Everybody tryna have a nice conversation, and you tryna talk about yo shit. It ain T world, man. Can't be that way."

Troy said, "What? Nah man."

"It ain only about you, T," Face said. "Can't care only about yoself." He pounded on the dumpster lid. "Ain T world, man."

"Nah, I'on't care about myself," Troy said, shaking his head a little and straightening his blankets. "I'on't care if I die tomorrow. Come on, I'ma bum. I'm fung bum, I don't care about myself. I'm nobody, y'know?"

"Aight man," Face said, staring off to the side. "I heard you, jo. Coo."

Troy said, "No, bissa, becussa I—"

"I said I heard you, motherfucker. Damn, shut the fuck up, Troy."

Face was tapping the dumpster lid with his fingernails. Making a fist with the other hand. Nobody said anything for a little bit.

We finished the fifth.

Face and Troy split a grape-flavored cigar.

I threw some rocks at a 'Slow' sign on a lightpole for a little bit then said goodbye.

Face shook my hand and patted my shoulder. "I'ma go too, cous. Tired of this assho."

But Troy was asleep again.

Where the alley broke off in different directions, Face and I went different directions.

He smashed the empty fifth against a garage.

The pit bull down the alley barked, 'Oorv oorv.'

THANK YOU FOR WAKING ME UP TODAY, JESUS

When I passed by Spider-Man's this afternoon the alley was cleared of his bed, shit from the dumpsters everywhere, rental cars parked against the brick wall.

So I went to Troy's.

Troy and Craig were leaning on a dumpster sharing a 40.

Troy pointed at me, opening and closing his mouth silently as if forgetting what to say.

He came out from behind the dumpster, excited to see me for some reason.

"And what is goin on, my man," he said.

We bumped forearms.

"Fuck yeah, Troy," I said.

"Run it," he said, pointing at me with both hands.

"I'm going to get some 40s. You guys want anything?"

"Yeah, if you could," Troy said, clasping his hands together.

I went across the street and got three 40s.

"Oh, shit, anks man," Troy said, when I handed him one.

Craig said, "Yeah, we could've shared one, me and Troy. But thank you."

We stood around drinking.

Talking about the Blackhawks.

Talking about bullshit.

Every once in a while Troy would look at me and say, "How *you* feelin?"—pointing at me and silently moving his mouth, paste all around his lips.

And I'd say, "I'm good, Troy."

And then he'd point at Craig and say, "And how *you* feelin?"

And Craig would say, "Wimma hands, man."

Down the alley, a garage door opened.

This lady came out.

She was holding a smashed-looking 12-pack.

She and Troy seemed to know each other.

They said hi.

"Here, you guys can have this beer," she said. "I don't want it."

She set the case on top of a dumpster.

"Thank you," I said.

"No problem," she said. She put some hair behind her ear and folded her arms. "It's been in my fridge for like, a year now."

Troy said, "Well aright! Run it!"

The woman laughed and said, "Ok guys" and waved and went back into her garage, closing the door.

We finished our 40s then started on the case she'd brought us.

Behind the dumpsters at Troy's place.

The sun.

The smell of Troy's grape-flavored cigar.

Chicago, the land of fine sun and even finer grape-flavored cigars.

Welcome.

Craig walked off to the side of a garage to piss.

From behind the garage, he laughed and said, "Man, Troy, I's just thinking, remember when they had the drunk tank at the

Cali Ave. Po-lice Department?"

"Ha, yeah," Troy said. "I's in that bitch a hunnerd fucking times, man. Run it!"

Craig said, "Yeah so one time I's in there with Face and Danny. We got picked up by the park, all wasted and shit. They put us in nearby cells." He came back over, zipping his pants. "They hooked it *up* with them bologna sandwiches, man. Tellin you. Face ate like six them bitches and fell right asleep. Fucking Danny, he used the bread to wipe his ass."

We all laughed.

Craig said, "The cops cleared us and shit, but then they's like, something about staying a while longer because it was raining out. We all like, 'Hell no.' Didn't even wait for our shoelaces, man. Was only drizzling out too."

Troy said, "Aw man, at reminds me. Danny was around the other day, man. I'n't tell you."

"Aw shit," Craig said, smiling. "How is he?"

"Doin good, doin good," Troy said. "Heece walkin now. Came around and said what's up, gave us ten dollars for some beers. Run it. Still stayin with his pops and stepmom. Got a big belly now, big beard. Lookin good, man."

"Hell yeah," I said.

"Hell yeah," Troy said. "Run it."

We were quiet for a while.

The sun returned.

The heat and humidity increased.

Craig sniffed a few times and made a face, put his shirt over his nose. "Man. Smell like dookie and piss back here, Troy. The fuck."

Troy said, "What? Nah."

"Yeah, Troy. This shit bad. You fucked up."

"Nah, I clean up back here every week."

"Nah Troy, nah," Craig said. "Smell like dookie and piss." He turned to me, making eye contact with his shirt still over his nose. "Dookie and piss?"

"Yeah," I said.

"Aw, f'real?" Troy said.

"Yeah," I said. "Right when he said it, I smelled it."

Troy got up and walked around. "It does," he said. "Fuck. I'm sorry. I'm lazy. I'll clean up soon. Sorry guys. Only started making my bed once I became homeless, hah. Been in a house, been married, never made my bed. Now, I make my bed."

Nobody said anything for a little bit.

Troy apologized numerous times.

Said he was going to get the hose and bucket from the little co-op he worked at so he could clean his place.

He promised.

"I do the windows over here for these guys once a week and I'll just take the hose out here and spray it all down real good. Geez. I'm sorry guys. I'm lazy. Haven't even made a bed until I was homeless, hah."

Craig said, "That's on you, T."

This guy came around the corner, pushing a shopping cart full of cans and metallic garbage.

"Yo, Scrappy!" Craig said.

Scrappy parked his shopping cart and went behind the dumpsters.

Troy got up and arranged a different dumpster—one on wheels—to shield him some more.

"Hi, I'm Martin," he said to me, only part of his face visible behind the dumpster.

He was wearing a Bears hat pushed back on his head.

He had a very quiet and muted voice and he didn't blink at all.

"Am I gonna be cool?" he said to Troy, taking out a crackpipe.

Troy said, "Yeah yeah, don't worry. Save me a hit too."

Martin plunged his crackpipe with a small screwdriver and talked about making a lot of money off aluminum cans from this recent street festival in K-Town.

He packed the crackpipe and smoked, rotating the pipe and watching with his eyes crossed.

He exhaled and put his hand over his face.

I said I was going to get more beer, asked what people wanted.

Craig said, "I'll split a King Cobra with Troy."

Troy said, "Yeah man, anks."

I asked Martin if he wanted anything.

"No, I don't drink," he said. "But maybe like, a 7-Up or something, sure."

I went and bought two King Cobras, a cinnamon bun, and a can of 7-Up.

I ate the cinnamon bun in three bites before I even crossed the street.

Back at Troy's, Martin was still sitting behind the dumpster, mumbling quietly and staring.

Troy had taken off his hoody, wearing a tanktop with an American flag in the middle, the words "The United States of America" above the flag, then beneath it, "Winner of back to back World Wars."

He sat on the edge of his bed holding the crackpipe.

He loaded a rock and took a hit, tilting his head back and raising the pipe.

Craig said, "Damn man, don't advertise."

Troy exhaled.

He looked at Craig. "So how *you* feelin man?"

Craig smiled and winked. "Wimma hands, man."

"Feel *this* with your hands," Troy said, motioning like he was going to unzip his pants.

"Fuckatta here, Troy," Craig said, laughing. "Kill you."

"No, whatta y'think," Troy said. "Issa, we can go to Boystown and make a quick 40 bucks. Handjobs. Anyone wanna go with?"

"You nasty," Craig said, shaking his head.

Troy said, "No, but ey, sometimes they just wissa, wanna watch you jack off. Easy money, man. Come on. Anybody?"

Craig said, "You fucked up, Troy. Fuckin dumbass."

Martin stood up from behind Troy's bed and got his shopping cart and left without saying anything, adjusting his hat as he walked away.

"Later Scrappy," Craig said.

Martin held up his hand.

Clouds had dimmed things a little.

Troy and Craig leaned on the dumpster and I sat on an overturned bucket.

We finished our beers.

A station wagon pulled into the alley and parked by us.

Three guys exited.

One of them knew Troy.

They worked for a church in the neighborhood.

They were delivering food in tied-off plastic shopping bags.

Troy got three bags off them and also a pair of pants.

"Anks so much, guys," Troy said, holding the pants up. "Great." He folded the pants over his arm. "So, where else you guys at tonight then?"

One guy said, "Just came to swing by here, then uh, think we're going down by the bridge and"—he looked at another guy.

The other guy said, "Yeah, I think that's it."

Troy told them about another place to go to drop off food, under a bridge by the river.

"Oh thanks, thank you," said a church employee. "So, you guys good tonight? Everything good?"

"Yeah," Troy said.

"Yeah," I said, waving my fist a little, like 'Hell yeah, man.'

Troy said, "Ey, really, anks for the food and everything. Real sorry, like, we been boozin and everything."

One of the church guys said, "No, don't worry about it."

Troy said, "Ey, come on, let's have a prayer before you guys leave. Here."

We all held hands in the alley.

On one side I was holding Craig's hand and on the other side I was holding one of the church guy's hands, on a dumpster lid.

A church employee started the prayer with, "Lord our Father, please continue to love and guide us. We thank you for the food you have given us to share."

Nobody said anything for a little bit.

The guy who started the prayer said, "Troy, you wanna—"

Troy cleared his throat. "Lord Jesus, thank you for wakin me up today."

There was a long pause.

A guy from the church said, "In Christ's name."

People said amen.

"Alright, later guys," said one of the guys from the church.

We all hugged before they got back in the car and drove off.

Craig squatted with his back against a dumpster, opening his bag.

Troy sat on his bed, opening a bag.

He picked up the unopened bag and handed it to me.

"Here man, have at it," he said.

"Oh, thanks," I said.

Each bag had two sandwiches, beef jerky, an apple, a juicebox, chips, and a bottle of water.

In a bag within the bag, there were shaving razors, deodorant, and hand sanitizer.

Troy immediately began to sort his stuff.

"Poppin Strawberry," he said, looking at the juicebox.

He gave me his extra sandwich and a bag of chips and an apple.

Craig was chewing, holding half a sandwich. "Troy, gimme that other sandwich, man."

"Nah man, I only got one. I gave the other one to him."

Craig looked at me. "Lemme get it, man."

I shook my head, laughing. "Oh my."

Craig smiled. "Come on, man."

He started proposing trades.

"I'm not really attracted to any of those offers," I said, unwrapping my sandwich.

Troy said, "Man, kinda feel bad bout all the Jesus shit since we been boozin. Smokin stones and shit."

Craig said, "Man, me too. Talkin bout prayin and shit and we out here all drunk—ackin stupid."

"Ah well," Troy said, opening a small bag of chips. He laughed a little and barked out some mucus. "God don't judge, y'know?"

We ate in silence.

The sandwich was some kind of lunchmeat between bologna and salami.

I liked it a lot.

To say I only liked it a little, this would be a lie.

Craig threw some tomato slices over his shoulder. "Man, these tomaters suck."

"'Tomaters?'" Troy said. "What is that, some nigger sh—hah, no pun intended."

Craig lowered his head, laughing.

He let his head hang for a second then looked up at Troy.

"Man, I got a fuckin job and a home and a wife and kids, and you out here." He pointed at Troy. "You stupid, Troy. You really stupid."

Troy laughed. "I know I know. I's just playin, man. Settle down, hah. I'm a fung bum, man. My place smells like dookie and piss for fuck sake. Don't lissna me."

Like all the things you like about someone are things you see in a way that makes them complimentary.

And all the things you dislike about someone, same.

I walked around the corner and pissed on a garage, backing up on tiptoe to avoid the puddle.

Said bye to Troy and Craig and got walking.

It began to rain.

And for a second, I thought it was my job—as appointed by the city—to be outside to like, greet the rain.

To welcome it.

And who better than me?

Fucking no one!

TENTS

This afternoon there was a voice message on my phone—from Spider-Man.

The message was choppy but I heard 'library' so I walked by the library and Spider-Man was out front, using the outlet to charge his phone.

"Ohhhh, wha's good man!" he said.

We hugged.

He kissed my cheek and said we should go meet up with Janet.

First we went to the 7/11 and got some King Cobras.

"What happened to your old spot?" I said, exiting the 7/11 and holding the door for him. "I haven't seen you."

"Dahhh. Man, I gave that shit up. We at Janet's so long, you know, the car rental place, they cleaned it up. Shit, you kiddin me? Did me a favor! I couldn't move them beds. Hell nah. You need some fuckin tools to clean that mess, nang! Needa fuckin crane, fuckin bulldozer."

I pictured a bulldozer pushing his bed away as he sat on it, holding onto the sides yelling, "Gah be kiddin me!"—Janet speeding behind in her wheelchair.

"But nah, we over this way now," he said, pointing somewhere.

We walked to a vacant lot near a different section of the Blue Line tracks.

The ground was mostly rocks and glass.

They were living up against a brick wall with a mural spraypainted on it.

Janet lay on her side in a sleeping bag, playing a game on her cellphone.

Ten feet away I saw an adult diaper stained with shit and blood, a pinched wad of bloody gauze next to it.

I sat on the rocks and glass, hands in my pockets to keep warm.

It was October and getting cold already.

"Yeah, we only stayin here like, two weeks though," Spider-Man said.

He rested a piece of luggage up against the wall and sat on it.

They were moving to Las Vegas on Halloween.

They'd have Janet's disability checks and Spider-Man would try to get his job back cleaning up hotels and casinos.

"Last time I's there," he said, "I had a job and an apartment the first day. First fucking day, du."

He mimed unsheathing a sword from his back and went, "Shiiiiiiing…fuckatta here."

He showed me the things they'd be taking with—two pieces of luggage, a reusable grocery bag, and two sleeping bags.

Without looking up from her game, Janet said, "Buh, beb. Ya bitch is hungry. Hehe. Shit. Dayum."

Spider-Man reached into his hoodie pocket and took out a 7/11 deli sandwich, halved and stacked in cellophane.

"Ok," he said, "but it's just 7/11 sandwiches."

Janet rolled over onto her stomach, reaching for the sandwich.

The sleeping bag unzipped a little.

She was naked from the waist down.

She moaned a little, "Ahh, beb, shit, fock. Ahhh. Hep, peez."

Spider-Man took her hand and helped turn her over as he read the back of the sandwich package.

"They put so much shit innem now," he said. "I don't even know half this shit—fucking enzymes and shit. Fucking CO_2 or some shit haha. The fuck!?"

I was looking at the mural spraypainted on the brick wall.

It had aliens wearing basketball jerseys DJing records that were pizzas, hearts with keyholes in them floating through outerspace, dinosaurs holding bow and arrows, floating hands dropping sand, the moon, rockets, swirls, cats.

Spider-Man told me about how he was there when the community helped artists paint the wall a few years ago.

Everybody set up a little camp in the lot, and they grilled and spent time with other families in the neighborhood.

"I mean yeah, we're going to miss everybody," he said. "Our first trip back probably won't be for a long time, but—it's whatever."

Janet said some things about what Las Vegas would be like— as though repeating things Spider-Man had told her many times.

"Ey, there's Keith," Spider-Man said. He pointed to the alley across the lot. "KEITH! EY, KEITH!"

Keith was walking through the alley, trying to balance with his head down.

I'd heard Spider-Man and others talk about Keith.

Something about not smoking Keith's weed.

Something about PCP.

Embalming fluid dipped joints.

Walking around talking to streetlights.

Something something.

Something about how he's banned everywhere.

The 7/11, the liquor store, fucking outerspace.

Man, Keith banned from the fuckin galaxy!

"Keith!" Spider-Man yelled again. "Ey Keith!"

Keith kept walking.

"He got his headphones on," Spider-Man said.

He threw some rocks.

Nothing.

"I'ma go get him," Spider-Man said, ran off.

I asked Janet about the stuffed animals in the back pouch of her wheelchair—a blue bear and a little orange cat staring at me.

Janet said, "Wuh, one is called Bluey, and um, the other, Ms. Meow Meow."

She formally introduced me to both, speaking for them.

I said hello, waving to each as they waved to me.

We had a short, polite conversation during which we discovered that everyone was having a nice day.

Janet apologized for them both being dirty and said they were going to get baths before they left, along with everything else they were bringing.

"Yeah," I said, looking into the all-white eyes of Ms. Meow Meow. "Yeah."

Spider-Man and Keith came back.

Keith was drunk as fuck, sipping liquor from a small plastic orange-juice container and laughing like 'guh guh guh.'

He had slicked-back gray hair and a boiled-looking face with deep wrinkles.

He wore a leather coat, sweater, dress pants and dress shoes.

He had very small, perfectly straight teeth, except for one front tooth that looked like a drop of spit coming out of his gumline.

I kept expecting it to fall out.

He started talking like, "Yeah no…no yeah, I mean, no because…."

Eventually he told us about some tents he'd seen in a nearby alley, said we should go grab them.

"Yeah no, I mean I got these tents," he said. "They're in this one yard. No but I, see there was, shit I gotta go to sleep. But no, there's tents, I got tents. I woke up too early though, and I gotta, I gotta go to sleep now."

"How long they been there?" Spider-Man said.

"I mean no," Keith said. "Onissly, I think yeah, maybe two or three nights or somethin."

"Oh, what?" Spider-Man said, relighting the cigarette in his mouth. "They ain gonna be there then. Hellllll to the motherfuckin nah."

I stared idly at the cherry on his cigarette before turning to look at Keith.

Keith had put in plastic vampire teeth.

He bit at me, opening his eyes real big.

And for a second, it genuinely scared me.

Like my heart beat faster and I almost jumped at him.

But then the teeth fell out a little.

Keith, you silly bastard.

I can see why you're banned in outerspace!

…the fucking galaxy!

"Let's go get the tents," I said.

"Nah, they won't be there," Spider-Man said, shaking his head. "Shit."

Keith still had the vampire teeth in, kind of.

He made a serious expression. "Hey but no, who knows, man. But onissly though, I have to go to sleep, so, let's va-moose."

Spider-Man and I left to go get the tents.

Keith gave us vague instructions, following far behind, trying to keep up.

At one point, we lost him.

But then he came out from behind a parked car and made a scary face at us with the plastic vampire fangs in his mouth—both hands up high over his head, walking wide-legged for some reason.

"He always cross the street in the middle," Spider-Man said, laughing. "I'on't know, he likes them thrills I guess."

We went down an alley.

Keith showed us the backyard.

"They're in, um—they're over there," he said.

He was laughing, trying to keep the vampire teeth in his mouth.

He walked down the alley, yelling something about needing to go to sleep.

Spider-Man went into the backyard and grabbed a duffle bag and a rolled-up tarp.

On the walk back, we discussed how nice the tent would be if we could get it set up, especially since it was going to rain.

We both agreed: it would be really nice.

I asked him how many points this mission would be worth, because sometimes he referenced things in terms of points, like a videogame.

"Dah, gotta be nuts. Fuckin, 50 thousand easy, du."

Back at the vacant lot, Janet was playing a game on her cellphone, music on loud.

"Yay," she said. "I, luh, luff camping, beb. Shit. Dayum. Heh."

Spider-Man and I tried to set up the tent and we almost completed it but then the last piece was broken.

Defeat.

Felt like I could've made the tent work somehow if I had like an hour to search the lot and nearby alleys.

But no.

Spider-Man said fuck it, he just wanted the tarps, to wrap him and Janet up at night…"human taco style."

He demonstrated with his hands, slapping them down over each other.

"Human taco," I said.

Janet turned over a little with her bare ass hanging out of the sleeping bag. "I wanna be a, a taco, beb. Shit. Heh."

Spider-Man had both palms up, slapping one down then the other on top.

"Shwoop shwoop," he said, laughing. "Wrapped up like a motherfucker!"

I said, "Oh, I met Ms. Meow Meow and uh, Bluey."

"Bloo-AY!" Spider-Man yelled. "Hayo yeah. Those her babies."

Janet reminded him he'd promised to get her a real dog when they settled in Vegas.

"You said, beb," she said.

Spider-Man nodded, looking at the ground.

"An a kitty," she said.

"Shit, I ain buyin no farm!" Spider-Man said, looking up. "Fuckatta here! What?!" He shook his head. "That's bananas."

Janet was laughing. "An a—a ham-ther peez."

Spider-Man made a face at me.

"A dog, a kitty, *and* a hamster," I said.

Janet laughed.

Spider-Man told me about a hamster he bought his oldest daughter when she was very young (she was now my age).

"Mr. Wiggles," Spider-Man said, smiling. He reached down and picked up a bottle cap. "Shit, he's no bigger than this when we got him. What!? Are you *high*?!"

I was smiling.

I already liked Mr. Wiggles.

Wanted to know everything about him: from basic history on through the entire lineage of his thoughts.

"Shit, I did everything for his happy lil ass," Spider-Man said. "I built him a mansion, fuckin everything." He described the layout of the hamster mansion. "That shit was like, this tall"—hand by his waist, "and this wide"—hands maybe three feet apart. "There were two places to eat, four places to sleep, shit, three bathrooms, motherfuckin tubes, slides, whistles, a hot tub an a motherfuckin tennis court. Wha's really going on?"

I adjusted my ass on the rocks and glass, picked up a hooked piece of glass and threw it.

The sky was gray, air smelled like rain.

"Mr. Wiggles, man we loved that little guy," Spider-Man said. "He was like a dog, bro. Shit, we'd put him out in his plastic ball and he'd follow my daughter around. He'd go by the door when she left for school and just stay by the door for a long time, bro. Fuckatta here. Shit, Mr. Wiggles lived that life, man. He lived seven years! Seven years!" He looked up and pointed at the sky. "We miss you, Wiggles!" Then he looked at me and slapped his thigh, mimed like he was holding a videogame controller. "I'd take him out of his ball and set him right here in my lap, play my videogames. He'd sit on my lap for hours. Man, he had it all. Best life a hamster could have. Fuckin bananas! But nah then my daughter, Josalie, she wake me up all cryin one day. I said, 'Oh boy.'" He whistled a note. "Mr. Wiggles had passed. So I call up my friends and like, seven people or so came over. Everyone had on suits and everything, what?! We took turns in the backyard diggin with this little garden shovel, haha, then everyone threw some dirt on him. I said the sermon bro! I said, 'Lord, we thank you for Mr. Wiggles and we know you'll take care of him now.' Maaaan, everybody was crying they eyes out. Nang! We put stones around his grave, everything. Everything for his happy lil ass. It was beautiful. Just beautiful, man. Shit man, he had everything. I even bought him a girlfriend." He made double ok signs with his hands. "'Mrs. Frederickson.' My daughter named her. I'on't know where she get these names from. But nah, her and Wiggles hated each other, du. She was cold, man! She was cold to Mr. Wiggles! She died after like, a year though, so whatever. And we ain do no big funeral for her I just put her in a cigar box, wrapped it in tape, and threw her ass in the garbage."

I laughed, looking at the rocks and glass.

"She'a cold bitch, man," he said again, opening his eyes wide and turning his head sideways a little. "I just tossed her."

It was getting windy.

I felt a few raindrops.

Janet showed Spider-Man her score on the cellphone videogame.

It was her highest score yet.

S'MORES

I saw Spider-Man and Janet out front of the library this afternoon.

Spider-Man was wearing big pajama pants, a winter vest, and a large plush tophat with the Superman logo on it.

He yelled, "Well lookie lookie"—dancing over with his fist out.

I bumped my fist against his.

Janet called me over for a hug. "Wuh, whay's my huggy? I, nuh, need my huggy!"

She was parked against the wall charging her wheelchair and playing blackjack on her phone.

She wore a giant knit winter hat that went over her eyes a little.

There were shit stains on the inner thigh area of her jeans and she smelled like s'mores.

I hugged her and stood next to her with my back against the wall.

Spider-Man was really drunk, walking around the front walkway.

He took out a small, thin-bladed knife and danced, tophat waving.

He came up to Janet and mimed cutting her legs off, humming to himself.

She laughed, saying, "Stop, stop"—trying to play her game.

"Why?" he said, making slicing motions just above her legs. "You don't need em."

He kept doing the slicing motion, humming to himself.

"They're still hers," I said.

Janet said, "Yeah, they still mine, beb."

Spider-Man smiled, raising his eyebrows up and down as he made cutting motions around her legs.

He put the knife in his vest pocket and walked around the front walkway of the library.

He came up to me and put his hand on my shoulder.

He said, "All I'm sayin is, man, take a motherfucker, take away his weapons, his clothes, everything, and drop his ass off in the Amazon, see what happens. Go ahead. Stick him in there at the fuckin Nile. Dahhhh. That's bananas. That's nuts. Are you *high*!? Fuckin 25 foot crocodile eat that happy-ass in a heartbeat." He snapped his mouth closed and went, "Hahnnnnnnnn." He made a jaw motion with both his arms closing together. "25 feet bro! Come on! Are you *high*!?" He measured a 25 foot crocodile out on the sidewalk—using paces—then did the snapping motion with his arms. "Fuckin nuts, fucking bananas, woo."

It was cold out but very sunny, and sometimes I could only see Spider-Man as a negative, dancing around in the brightness.

"An there's a fuckin herd of em, bro!" he said. "A herd of fuckin giant-ass crocodiles layered underneath the water, just waitin man! You fuckin gotta be kiddin me!" He walked away a little bit and came back shaking his head, holding the brim of his tophat. "You ever see a motherfuckin wildebeest around them things? Shit. That shit's fuckin bananas."

He acted like a wildebeest.

He trotted up to an imaginary body of water and stopped, looking side to side and blinking his eyes a lot.

"They come up to the water—sip sip—hmmmm that's good. Look around, make sure no lions around and shit—sip sip—hmm, that's good. Hey guys, let's go!"

He waved the other wildebeests forward over his shoulder.

He walked around the front entrance area of the library, saying, "Ohhh-wowo. Ohhhhh-wowo. That's what they say, bro. Ohh-wowo."

Janet kept trying to show him her score in the videogame but he ignored her.

"Trivia," he said, clasping his hands together with both his forefingers to his lips. "Lobsters, crab, shrimp and krill: what are they?"

"Crustaceans?" I said.

"No, insects. Six legs. Fuckin exoskeleton. *And* they lay eggs."

Spider-Man did an egg-laying motion.

He squatted down and put his hands on his hips, saying, "Pip pip pip."

I was laughing.

He continued to do it, looking side to side.

He grabbed his 40 and drank the last of it in a few pulls.

Then he licked his lips, blinking his eyes. "Hmm, spicy!"

Janet laughed, slouching forward in her chair.

Spider-Man did the egg-laying motion again, extending his ass with his hands on his hips.

"Pip pip pip." He stood up. "Shit bro, that's like the motherfuckin tarantula hawk. You heard about this bitch?"

"Have I heard about the tarantula hawk?" I said.

He told me about the tarantula hawk.

"This some fuckin alien shit," he said. "Gah be kiddin me! It's a fucking wasp that attacks tarantulas man! Oohwee!" He made a face like he'd stubbed his toe. "That shit's like four inches long bro"—gesturing with his fingers out, thumbs end-to-end. "You kiddin me?!" He started pacing a little, shaking his head. "Are you *high*!? Fucking tarantula hawk swoop down"—he motioned with his one hand like he was dive bombing, made the other hand into a crawling spider, "stings—shish, shish. Meanwhile this guy's biting—narsh narsh—sting, bite, sting, bite, fuuuucckkk!! It's bananas. That's totally bananas, man. Tony bananas. After a few stings, that spider's done, man. Fuckatta here. Then the tranchula hawk carries the motherfucker back to the nest, where there's already a hole and drops that motherfucker in." He chopped one hand into the other hand. "LAYS EGGS ON THE MOTHERFUCKER"—pauses, staring at me—"pip pip pip, then covers em back up and leaves. So when the eggs hatch they got something to eat before they climb out the ground and fly away." He made a 'twinkling' motion with his fingers going up to the sky. "What!?" He paced away, pointing at me. "That's nuts man. That's some alien shit." He turned around. "You wanna tell me we came here from a man and woman!? Hahhhh, nah du. Nah, that's some outerspace shit. Some alien shit. Fuck that."

Janet said, "Fock dat. Heh. Dayum."

The front of her vest was dark with drool.

She took some lipstick out of her pocket, told me she stole it from a pharmacy.

"I, um, I only take, luh, little things."

"She a klepto, man!" Spider-Man said. "She see something, she take it. She *have* to take it. Shit. That's what a klepto is man!"

Janet applied some lipstick.

Spider-Man told her to rub her lips together, demonstrating himself with his hands on his hips.

Janet was looking at me, pushing her lips out with her eyes closed.

"Do—do it look, good?" she said.

"Yeah, it looks nice," I said.

She laughed, opening her eyes.

Then she hiccupped, front teeth biting down over her bottom lip.

"Wait, why you puttin lipstick on?" Spider-Man said, folding his arms. "Who you tryna kiss?"

"Yuh, you beb!" she said. "Shit."

Spider-Man danced up to her and they kissed.

He told me more about Janet's crimes.

She was laughing the whole time.

He told me about how he and Janet and his friend Tony used

to steal DVDs from video rental places.

Tony was also in a wheelchair.

Spider-Man would go into a videostore pushing him, acting like they didn't know Janet, who'd go in a few minutes later.

Then Tony would knock over a display case and Spider-Man would apologize to the employees and help them clean it up while Janet put stacks of DVDs in her wheelchair and left— Spider-Man and Tony following soon after.

All in all they stole about 300 DVDs at different places.

I was laughing.

Spider-Man said, "Nah, but man, Tony, he was my best friend, man. I loved him. He just died like—shit—three days ago."

His eyes got a little more red and watery.

When I asked what happened, Spider-Man just said Tony had gotten really sick, had sores on his legs all the way into the bone, couldn't breathe.

"His body just didn't wanna do it anymore," he said. "But nah, he ok now."

He explained how Tony was in a wheelchair since the age of 10, when he got shot in the head by a stray bullet.

Spider-Man looked at Janet. "He knew what it was like to walk, see? He remembers. You don't. You couldn't even dream about it because you never knew. See?"

Janet ignored him, playing blackjack on her phone again, the music loud.

I smelled s'mores.

She looked up and said, "Oh, shuh, shit. Fock dat." She looked at me. "No, doe worry. Iss, muh, my problem. Shit."

She backed into the wall a few times, made a few wrong turns, then used the automatic door and went inside the library.

Spider-Man sat in the woodchips and plugged in his phone, started playing a game.

The music was funny.

Quest music.

Made my heart beat harder.

Made me want to quest so bad.

Fuck yeah.

Any quest.

Me and whoever.

Me by myself.

I don't care if I die.

If I go on a quest and it kills me, oh well, that's how I want it.

I sat down in the woodchips next to Spider-Man.

"Love this game," he said, sniffing a few times. "Called *Blood Brothers*. You gotta run through valleys and shit, fuckin fight monsters and snakes. Scrazy man. Fuckin bananas. I got this fuckin sword, you gotta be kiddin me! Fuckin crystal sword, dahhhh."

He showed me the screen.

Couldn't tell what I was looking at.

He started playing again and I listened as he detailed the plot of the game, including main bosses.

Many of the bosses sounded impossible to beat.

And yet, here he was, beating them.

I saw a day-old daily paper under the bushes.

I looked through it without reading anything—eventually just laying the paper open on my lap and staring at some birds on a powerline.

Fuck yeah.

Spider-Man tapped the paper, saying, "That's some fucked-up shit, man. They finally sentenced his ass."

It was a story from a few years ago when this guy in the neighborhood ran up behind two women and hit them both in the head with a baseball bat, damaging the one girl to where she'd never talk again.

The attacker was sentenced to 120 years.

"Oh yeah, I remember this," I said.

"*Fuck* that punk," Spider-Man said, pointing down with his bent-up finger. There was snot coming out of his nose. "Fuck that motherfucker. That's some bitch shit, du. Fuckin pussy! Man they better relocate his ass to a different state, du. If he serves around here, they'a kill his ass *right* away. Fucking pussy bitch. I wish he try that shit on me. Bring that bat here, motherfucker. You get one swing." He held up one finger. "Then I fucking *kill* you."

I imagined myself as a public executioner for the city of Chicago.

One who used a baseball bat to execute prisoners.

I'd live in a tower somewhere out in Lake Michigan, within a few miles of the city.

And on the night of the execution they'd send a boat for me and I'd have to go ashore and kill someone with a baseball bat.

Spider-Man discussed the treatment of certain kinds of criminals in prison—like rapists or pedophiles or punks.

The treatment was beatings, stabbings, burnings, rapes, and murder.

"Specially if you hurt them kids, bro," he said, shaking his head with his eyes closed. "You hurt some kids they cold eat your ass, man." He started laughing and made a saluting gesture with his hand. "They'a eat your fuckin ass. They say, 'Ok, you want to hit some girls with a baseball bat? Ok. Alright.'"

He mimed raping someone with a broomstick or bat-like object, doing a motion with one hand like he was breaking a game of pool over and over again.

"Yeah motherfucker, run that shit," he said, snarling and clamping his teeth. "Run, that, shit."

He kept doing the motion.

I was laughing.

What a nice day.

A day to ask for forgiveness in advance, for whatever.

A day to quest for forgiveness.

I read a random line in the article about how the attacker made a 'puppy-dog' face to his family in court when the judge read the sentence.

"Tellin you, bro," Spider-Man said, tapping the article again. "They better relocate his ass or he dead. Just like they did with Dahmer. Oohwee. Cold smashed his ass. Fuckin bananas."

He did a little inhalation through his front teeth like 'sssssss.'

Then he explained how Dahmer died, resting his phone in his lap, dulling the quest music.

"A guard took his ass to 'clean a bathroom,'" Spider-Man said, doing the quotes. "Then the guard left, and four dudes came in and smashed him. Cold smashed his ass. They don't give a fuck. They all lifers anyway. What's 45 more years? Who give a fuck? Fuckin fists, kicks, broomsticks, stompin his ass. Bashed his head against the toilet. Dahhh."

He mimed slamming his own head into a toilet, hand on the back of his neck.

"Goosh goosh goosh, ahhhhh," he yelled, making a cartoonish face.

He was sucking in the spit that came out over his lips, in between laughing and saying, "Goosh goosh."

"Ayo yeah, man," he said. "You kiddin me? Blood everywhere. On the toilets, the sinks, the mirrors. Blood on the fuckin ceiling, man. What!? Are you high?"

I was smiling.

Felt a painful excitement in my chest and stomach.

Like everything was perfect for me at that moment.

Blood all over the ceiling of my life.

Blood everywhere.

A quest for blood everywhere.

If not blood everywhere, then nowhere.

Keith walked by.

He came over and asked for a dime.

I gave him one.

"Yeah I jus woke up," he said. "Man." He stared at us for a second. "Went to sleep at like ten this morning, but no because I mean, this morning I got too fucked up, so. Hey but no, you going to Tony's funeral tonight?"

"Nah man, hell nah," Spider-Man said. "Not goin to that shit."

Keith said, "No because, anyway, I have to go to sleep I guess. I'll see ya."

He walked away.

The door to the library opened and Janet came out.

Spider-Man said he refused to go to his friend Tony's funeral because he wanted to remember him how he was, "…smiling, laughing, hugging, playing."

Same with his mom, his brother, his sister.

"No," he said, loud. "No way. I'm not going to that shit. Funerals are stupid. Man, just fuckin burn me. Don't fuckin waste time on making me look fake, fuckin, makin my family sad, buyin an expensive box. Fuck allat. You don't even have to make it special with the ashes. Thow em in the lake, the fuckin park, I don't care."

"Yeah, just pour me down the sewer," I said, watching traffic for a second.

"Yeah, the sewer," he said, shrugging, like 'sure, why not.'

I said what if one or more of your relatives used your ashes to do a homemade tattoo.

And then when s/he died, same thing.

So in a thousand years, your great-great-great-whatever would have part of his great-great-great-whatever inside his/her body as a decoration.

Janet said she wanted to be cremated and worn in a necklace around Spider-Man's neck.

It took her a long time to explain herself, which annoyed Spider-Man.

He kept referencing her 'batteries.'

"Damn, ey, where the batteries at?" he said, checking around her wheelchair.

Or he'd try to unplug a plug of hers.

"Should I unplug this? Boop."

Janet laughed a little.

"How about this?" he said. "Boop."

"Stop, beb. Stop."

A woman and child exited the library.

They walked up to the street, holding hands.

The child had a small head that looked bent down the middle, bowing outward. He yelled "Eh…eh," pointing at the street with his free hand.

"Downs Syndrome," Spider-Man said, looking from the kid to me, nodding. "He got Downs Syndrome."

The kid with Downs Syndrome stood by the street, yelling, "Eh, eh"—pointing at cars.

Spider-Man watched.

"He got Downs Syndrome," he said. "That's ok though. Nothin wrong with that. That's how he talks to the cars, right? He sayin, 'Hey, let me cross.' That's how he talks to them."

"Yeah," I said.

I smelled s'mores.

SUNBEAM SWORD

I saw Spider-Man at his old spot beneath the train tracks tonight.

It was warm out and raining very hard, the night before Halloween.

Spider-Man was in his vest and pajama pants and black plush tophat—suitcases by his side and a 40 resting on the hood of a rental car.

He raised his arms and came up and hugged me, pressing his forehead into my forehead.

We were both soaked.

"I thought that's you," he said, patting my shoulder. "Oh man."

His eyes were puffy and there were green plugs of mucus in the corners, paste around his mouth.

Told me he'd been kicked out of the library and couldn't go back until it closed.

"Where's Janet?" I said.

He didn't know.

He shrugged and pinched his nose to clear some rain.

"Should we go find her?" I said.

"Nah," he said. "She'a find me." He shook his head. "I can't ever find her ass, but she *always* find me. I go to fuckin Italy, fuckin Venice, hide under the docks, she come up knockin, doof doof doof, 'Hell-ooooooo?'"

The rain was slowing.

I asked if he wanted beer or cigarettes or food.

"Yeah I need a fuckin square, man," he said. He raised both fists to the train tracks and sky above, dripping water on him. "Need a square now motherfucker, what!?"

We went to the 7/11.

On the walk there, Spider-Man told me about these two kids who fucked with him last night out front of the library and how he chased them.

"Man, I will fuck you up," he said—to the kids from last night—raising his chin up as we crossed the street. "I will break your motherfuckin ass. Make you my sandwich. No mayo, no nothing. White bread, rye bread, whatever. Just you in my motherfuckin sandwich."

We entered the 7/11 and wiped our feet off on the rug—both of us soaked and smelling like dogs.

We went to the back of the store.

Spider-Man was still threatening the kids from last night, turning them into sandwiches.

"Nahhn," he said, doing a biting motion with his teeth, pulling his head back. "Fuckin eat that shit up."

I opened the glass door in front of him as he continued to mime a chewing motion.

I grabbed two 40s, feeling peace as the bottles behind them clinked forward.

Yes, hello.

I bought the 40s and a pack of cigarettes.

Spider-Man had a small electronic keycard thing on his necklace chain and he swiped it on a small display in front of the register.

He got points with purchases.

He checked his points on the screen, scrolling through what

he could get for 70 points.

At 100, he got a travel coffee container.

He expressed interest in the travel container, but—as he showed me with more scrolling—for 15,000 points, he got 2 hours for him and 20 friends to ride around in the company van drinking Slushees.

It was called 'The Brain Freeze Package.'

"Me, you—fuckin anybody," he said. "We drive around drinking as many Slushees as we can handle man, shiiiit, you in?"

"You're never going to get 15,000 points," I said, paying the cashier. "Never."

He laughed. "Fuckin A. Fuckin bananas."

He grabbed the cigarettes and started packing them.

We walked back to the alley and leaned on the hoods of rental cars, drinking our 40s.

There was a gang tag on a train track column.

Spider-Man tapped it with his 40 and talked about how gangbangers were pussies now.

"Straight bullshit, man, fuckatta here. Stealin and killin in your own neighborhood? What!? Are you high? Should be protecting your neighborhood—protecting your city."

He talked about how he gangbanged for the Insane Deuces when he was younger and how a rival in the Simon City Royals shot and killed three of his friends.

"Little scrawny ass motherfucker with a gun, man," he said. "We didn't play that gun shit back in the day, man. Hayo nah." He got off the car and paced around, waving his hand and shaking his head. He stopped and pointed at me, "That shit was pussy shit, man. You used your hands, or a bottle, or chain, bat, knife. No guns." He grabbed his bent-up nose and said, "Where you think I got this? Or this"—lifting up his shirt and showing me some stab wounds.

So he and two guys from different gangs—the Latin Kings and the Maniac Latin Disciples—got together and killed the guy who shot his friends.

They found out where he lived and attacked him on his back porch.

Spider-Man made punching and kicking motions.

His tophat wobbled and swayed.

A train was coming.

He seemed to remember something.

"Oh man," he said, and touched his face, grimacing, "That shit…."

He walked over to the concrete foundation of a train track column.

As a train went by overhead—cancelling all sound—he made a motion as if pounding the guy's face into the concrete over and over, yelling something.

He bent down at the knees a little and motioned with both his hands.

The train was gone.

"Then I grabbed that motherfucker by the throat," he said, teeth clenched. "I choked the shit out him. He was blue, totally blue, couldn't fucking make a sound. You kiddin me? And I said, 'You remember Buddy? Psycho? Cowboy? Huh?' He kept tryna to breathe, but the blood was all over. And I said, 'Fuck you.'"

He made a motion like he was dropping the guy, kicking his head one last time.

They left him dead on his back porch, strangled, his head smashed in.

"Me and the other du's, we hooked em up," Spider-Man said, gesturing like him and two other people were making a triangle with their arms, "We made the triangle, bing bing, and everybody left." He walked a few steps one way, pointing—"One guy went this way." Then he walked a different direction, pointing. "Another guy went this way." He pointed a different way, "I went this way. Never saw either of them again. And I don't regret it, man. Hayo nah I don't."

Janet rolled up right as her battery died.

"Shit, dayum. Fock dat. Heh."

"Ey, there she is," Spider-Man said.

She was soaked, wearing a candy necklace.

Said she'd been at Troy's, and that Troy had given her the candy necklace.

Spider-Man grabbed the necklace and kept trying to bite it but she slapped at his hand.

"Shut up, beb," she said. "Um, can I've a cigarette, peez?"

Spider-Man put a cigarette in her mouth and lit it for her.

I watched Janet smoke her cigarette, her head wobbling—saying, "Shit, damn, fock dat" on repeat as Spider-Man bit off pieces of her necklace and made suggestions about what he'd do to Troy if Troy stole her from him.

Things with scissors.

Things with bricks.

Look out, Troy!

Janet kept saying, "Ok, ok. Shut up, beb."

She went to flick her cigarette and it fell into her lap, burning her sweatpants.

Spider-Man told her to drop her cigarettes off to the side and not try any 'fancy flickin things.'

He kept grabbing her hand.

"Over here, ok!?" he said. "Over here!"

"Ok, ok," she said, trying to pull her hand back.

We stood around drinking, listening to the swish of rush hour traffic in the rain.

The trains above, more frequent, each time sending down older rainwater off the tracks onto my head and neck and back.

An ambulance and firetruck passed with sirens on.

Spider-Man jogged out to the edge of the alley and checked their identifying numbers.

"Both of them #3," he said. "That's over on Shakespeare and California. Right by where my mom used to live."

He talked about how his mom used to make cookies every Sunday for the firemen and policemen.

Firemen and policemen would line up at her house on

Sunday to get a cookie.

"She'd draw em like pigeons," Spider-Man said. "Man, one time—"

But then he started crying.

He walked away a little, pinching his eyes.

Then he came back and told a story about firemen stopping traffic when he and his mom were walking home from the grocery store, to get out and hug him and his mom.

Janet said how they used to live with Spider-Man's mom, and how much they loved each other.

"She, um, change my diaper. I say, 'You no have to do it, Janny be back soon.' But she, didda for me. I, wuh was embarrass, because no one see my, my privates. My, um, vuh—"

She looked at Spider-Man.

"Vagina," he said, sniffing. "Yes, that's what you have."

Janet looked back and me. "Um, yeah, my vagina. Heh. Shit."

Spider-Man was still crying, looking to the side and shaking his head.

But then he ate a few more pieces off Janet's candy necklace and seemed to feel better.

He checked the time on his phone and asked if I could push Janet to the library.

He wanted to go to the library to charge all their stuff before they left the next day.

I handed Janet my 40 and tucked her stuffed animals more securely into the back pouch of her wheelchair.

I pushed her out of the alley and onto the sidewalk.

It was raining hard again.

We were completely wet in seconds.

Janet joked about stealing my drink.

"I gonna, heh, I gonna, steal it," she said, holding the 40 closer to herself.

"Don't steal it," I said.

She laughed and said, "I luh, luff you."

I pinched rain out of my nose. "Yeah?"

She quietly said, "No, I mean it. I do."

When we got to the library, I parked her underneath the front entrance overhang.

Spider-Man came running up, wheeling the luggage.

"Oohweee," he said, shaking off.

He took off his tophat and slapped it a few times.

He put their luggage beneath some bushes, setting the sleepingbags under the overhang.

I sat down crosslegged and drank my 40.

Janet took out her stuffed animals and petted them.

We hung out drinking until really late, talking about what they had to do when they got to Las Vegas, playing trivia, yelling at people who walked by in costumes, trying to throw our bottlecaps against each other, pissing in the bushes, laughing.

I told Spider-Man and Janet I would miss them and to call me whenever they came back.

Eventually they went to sleep in their sleeping bags.

I sat there for a little bit then got up and walked home.

By the time I got near my place, it was getting light out.

Sunbeams were coming down from the bottom of the cloudcover, pointing to different areas of Chicago.

And I wanted to break off a sunbeam right where it met with the clouds and use it as a sword to protect the city.

Anyone coming in comes through me.

Anyone leaving leaves through me.

Anyone not wanted, denied.

Everyone else inside safe—but always in view of my sunbeam sword as I hold it, arms crossed and expressionless.

Also Available from Lazy Fascist Press

Go to work and do your job. Care for your children. Pay your bills. Obey the law. Buy products. by Noah Cicero

The Collected Works of Noah Cicero Vol. I by Noah Cicero

The Collected Works of Scott McClanahan Vol. I by Scott McClanahan

Anatomy Courses by Blake Butler and Sean Kilpatrick

Gil the Nihilist: A Sitcom by Sean Kilpatrick

The Laughter of Strangers by Michael J Seidlinger

American Monster by J.S. Breukelaar

Basal Ganglia by Matthew Revert

Motherfucking Sharks by Brian Allen Carr

A Pretty Mouth by Molly Tanzer

Broken Piano for President by Patrick Wensink

The Devil in Kansas by David Ohle

Zombie Sharks with Metal Teeth by Stephen Graham Jones

The Driver's Guide to Hitting Pedestrians by Andersen Prunty

and many more!